"Dammit, we should get married! You're pregnant! I'm the father!" Caleb roared.

Glory stared at him, and he could tell she was almost as shocked by the suggestion as he was.

"Do you realize you just proposed to me in the ladies' room?"

"It was expedient," Caleb gritted out.

Glory shook her head and laughed. "Oh, well, that's a terrific reason to spend the rest of your life with someone. Because it's expedient."

Caleb's chest felt like it was in a vise. For once he wished he had some experience with explaining his emotions.

Glory's gaze met and locked with his. Her blue eyes searched his for something. Caleb wondered if she found it.

She pressed her lips together and sighed. "You don't love me," she said quietly. "The answer is no."

Dear Reader,

Weddings, wives, fathers—and, of course, Moms—are in store this May from Silhouette Special Edition!

As popular author Susan Mallery demonstrates, Jill Bradford may be a *Part-Time Wife*, but she's also May's THAT SPECIAL WOMAN! She has quite a job ahead of her trying to tame a HOMETOWN HEARTBREAKER.

Also this month Leanne Banks tells a wonderful tale of an *Expectant Father*. In fact, this hero's instant fatherhood is anything but expected—as is finding his true love! Two new miniseries get under way this month. First up is the new series by Andrea Edwards, GREAT EXPECTATIONS. Three sisters and three promises of love—and it begins this month with *On Mother's Day*. Sweet Hope is the name of the town, and bells are ringing for some SWEET HOPE WEDDINGS in this new series by Amy Frazier. Don't miss book one, *New Bride in Town*. Rounding out the month is *Rainsinger* by Ruth Wind and Allison Hayes's debut book for Special Edition, *Marry Me, Now!*

I know you won't want to miss a minute of the month of May from Silhouette Special Edition. It's sure to put a spring in your step this springtime!

Sincerely,

Tara Gavin
Senior Editor

Please address questions and book requests to:
Silhouette Reader Service
U.S.: 3010 Walden Ave., P.O. Box 1325, Buffalo, NY 14269
Canadian: P.O. Box 609, Fort Erie, Ont. L2A 5X3

LEANNE BANKS

BANKS

EXPECTANT FATHER

Silhouette®

SPECIAL EDITION®

Published by Silhouette Books
America's Publisher of Contemporary Romance

Acknowledgments to: Richmond OB GYN, Bobbie Sunday, and some very special friends: Janet Evanovich, Bonnie Pega and Millie Criswell.

This book is dedicated to all the *grown-ups* who love *The Velveteen Rabbit* as much as I do.

 SILHOUETTE BOOKS

ISBN 0-373-24028-7

EXPECTANT FATHER

Copyright © 1996 by Leanne Banks

This edition published by arrangement with Harlequin Books S.A.

® and TM are trademarks of Harlequin Books S.A., used under license. Trademarks indicated with ® are registered in the United States Patent and Trademark Office, the Canadian Trade Marks Office and in other countries.

Printed in U.S.A.

Books by Leanne Banks

Silhouette Special Edition

A Date With Dr. Frankenstein #983
Expectant Father #1028

Silhouette Desire

Ridge: The Avenger #987

*Sons and Lovers

LEANNE BANKS

is a national number-one bestselling author of romance. Recognized for her sensual writing with a Career Achievement Award from *Romantic Times* magazine, Leanne likes creating a story with a few grins, a generous kick of sensuality and characters that hang around after the book is finished. Leanne's favorite hobbies include hugging her children, dancing with her husband in the privacy of their home and going out to dinner...any night will do.

VERY IMPORTANT MESSAGE

For _Caleb Masters_

From
M _s. Glory Danson_

Phone _(he knows the number)_
  Area Code   Number   Extension

Telephoned	☒	Returned your call		RUSH	
Came to see you		Please call		Special attention	☒

Message _Don't forget to pick up your suit from the dry cleaner._

P.S. You're going to be a father!

Chapter One

He was a public relations nightmare.

And he was all hers.

Glory Danson glanced over the file again and shuddered. She was *not* a miracle worker. Spying Pat Finch walking past her desk, she waved her over. Pat was Glory's last hope. She was tough and brassy, everything that Glory wasn't. "Pat, *you* like to travel. I bet you would love this assignment. Six cities in six weeks. I hear New Orleans is fun this time of year."

Pat lifted her eyebrows and ran her viper red fingernail over the file. She shook her head. "Never kid a kidder, hon," she said in her whiskey-and-cigarette voice. "I passed on this one last week."

"But he's a researcher for a drug that will help a lot of people. It's a great cause. The medical and human-interest media will eat this up."

"The media's the easy part. It's *him* that's the problem."

"He's a genius working on a drug for Alzheimer's."

"Admirable," Pat conceded. "Did you know they call him a research machine? That's the *nice* name. The people who don't like him call him the wild beast from the laboratory. I hear the director of the lab hasn't told this Masters guy that he's going to be on leave for a few weeks. He's trying to find the best time."

Glory's confidence wilted even more. She knew more about Caleb Masters than any file could tell, she thought, recalling her previous experience with him. "But think of the potential," she continued, desperately focusing on the positive. "He's young, extremely intelligent and single."

"His hair is longer than mine."

"He could get a haircut," she suggested.

Pat made a *tsk*ing sound. "Read the fine print, Glory. When he gets mad, he throws things. My five-year-old grandson knows better."

Glory bit her lip. "I don't suppose begging would help."

Pat shook her head and patted Glory's shoulder sympathetically. "I still don't understand why the boss handed this one to you."

"I asked for it," Glory said glumly. "But I didn't know what I was asking for. I told him I'd been doing press releases for the past six months and was ready to do more." She slapped the file closed in frustration. Where was her fortitude, her determination? Had her failed marriage stolen that from her, too? "I used to do image make-overs and media coaching without batting an eye before my marriage," she confided. "But looking at this, I feel like I'm headed into a war zone."

"Marriage will do that to you," Pat said, speaking from experience. "Suck you in and spit you out." She rummaged through her purse and put two business cards on Glory's desk. "Best bar in town. Take him there first, then to the haircutter. Chin up," she said as she left. "It's only six weeks."

Glory pushed her hair behind her ear and sighed. *Suck you in and spit you out.* How true. What had happened to the woman she'd been before she'd married Senator Richard Danson? Sometimes Glory looked in the mirror and wondered where her gumption had gone. Bright eyed and optimistic, ready to accept a challenge, full of confidence, her younger self had been eager and fearless until she'd fallen under the spell of the wealthy and charismatic senator. Who would have known Richard's perfectionist tendencies hid a streak of cruelty? Who would have known he could systematically destroy her confidence so that she would bend her will, always, to him?

She should have known.

That was the worst part. It had taken five years of tearing down to reach rock bottom, and secret visits to a women's center to scrimp together enough of her shredded courage to leave him. The marriage had been a total loss. She'd quit her job to please him, so she'd had to start near ground zero nine months ago. Worse, there'd been no precious children. Glory had always wanted children, but Richard had not.

Worst of all, Glory thought, she should have known. She should have seen the signs before she married. She shouldn't have made excuses for Richard. He hadn't wanted her. He'd wanted a human clay pot to mold and shape to his own delight. The problem was that his delight had changed, and she couldn't keep up.

So she'd lost more than money, more than her career and more than the chance to have babies. She'd lost the ability to trust herself, and she desperately wanted it back.

Glancing down at Caleb Masters's file again, she frowned. It was true that she'd had a negative experience working with Caleb many years ago. But if she'd been handed this before her marriage, before she'd lost her sense of self, what would she have done?

Swearing under her breath, she concentrated, trying to picture her reaction, but it was like trying to reach through a black hole. Her mind remained stubbornly blank. "Face it, Glory," she muttered. "You've got the PR job from hell."

"I've reassigned you out of the lab for the next six weeks," Dr. Jim Winstead said, his expression less resolute than his voice.

Caleb Masters stared across the desk in disbelief at the middle-aged man who was boss, mentor and friend. For a moment the only sound in the office was the clicking of Jim's ballpoint pen, one nervous habit he'd been unable to kick.

"You can't," Caleb finally said. Familiar restlessness bucked through him, driving him from the leather chair. "I'm so close to a breakthrough I can almost touch it. I can't take—"

Jim shook his head. "It's done. Another one of your co-workers found you sleeping at your desk when he came in at 6:00 a.m." His voice deepened in accusation. "You slept in the lab again."

Caleb sighed in irritation and scratched his unshaven jaw. "It was just one night."

"Three nights," Jim corrected bluntly, "within two weeks. We can't afford any mistakes."

Insulted, Caleb swore. "When have I made *any* mistakes? Hell, McAllister's made more mistakes than all of us put together, but I don't see you pulling him out."

"McAllister doesn't throw temper tantrums."

The statement lit the short stem of his temper. When had this incessant edginess inside him worn away his self-control? Caleb itched to throw the glass swan on Jim's desk out the window. Sucking in a calming breath, he narrowed his eyes. "Then why did you appoint me head of this research team if I'm such a pain in the butt?"

"That's easy." Jim grinned slowly. "Because you're a genius. When you get regular sleep and eat regular meals, you've got enough energy for five men. You motivate everyone around you to work far beyond their potential." Jim's grin faded. "But for the last few months you've been pushing too hard—" Jim held up his hand when Caleb tried to interrupt. "Everyone's afraid to say good-morning to you. Productivity is down."

A heavy weight settled in his chest. Caleb thought of his brother's messages on his answering machine that he hadn't returned. He remembered how he'd ignored Eli's warning that he was spending too much time in the lab. "And you think it's because of me."

Jim nodded. "Being a research scientist for a disease like Alzheimer's can bring out a superhero complex in any man. You've just got a bad case of it, and you don't have a wife or children to give you any perspective. You don't have the balance of—"

Caleb shook his head. He'd heard this spiel a dozen times before. "I've never bought into your theory of balancing work with leisure. I know where I get the biggest sense of satisfaction in my life, and it's when I take one step closer to finding a medicine that's going to add years to somebody's life. Somebody who's out of options." The fact that the clock was ticking for thousands of sick people, and that he was the last hope, was like a hot poker in his gut. "What could be more important?"

"It is important," Jim agreed. "But you've lost sight of the big picture, and we need you at top form back in the lab. That's why I'm temporarily reassigning you to the Speakers' Bureau."

"Speakers' Bureau!" Caleb shouted. He couldn't believe it. "You expect me to give speeches to a bunch of garden clubs for the next month?"

Jim's mouth twisted in irony. "I don't think the garden club is quite ready for you. No. I've got you on a traveling tour. You'll be speaking to political groups across the country, but it won't be a grueling schedule. Plenty of time for R and R. We're sending along a PR consultant to help with the press and anything else that comes up."

Caleb struggled with anger and defeat. The notion that he couldn't pour his energy into work that counted made him feel useless. Desperation hummed through him. "This is a waste. I could name ten guys who'd be better at public speaking. And I'm about as politically correct as toxic waste. I could end up doing the cause more damage than good."

Jim nodded. "You could, but you won't."

Caleb scowled. He didn't want Jim to be right. He didn't want to reassess his life and make changes. Making personal changes had always been difficult for him. Leaning forward, he planted his hands on Jim's desk and played his last card. "I could quit."

Jim went very still and took a deep breath. "You could. I hope you won't. I hope you'll see that I'm doing what I think is best for the project, the team and you."

Caleb rolled his eyes. He should have known Jim would know the exact words that would make him see reason. "Okay." He lifted his hands in defeat. "Six weeks and I'm back. When do I start?" He wanted to get it over with.

Jim clicked his pen again. "You start today. The PR expert will call you at home. Do some things you haven't done in a while. Smell the roses. Take a nap. Eat some decent food." His mouth lifted in a slight grin. "And for all our sakes here at the lab, get yourself a willing woman."

Cursing Jim's sick sense of humor, Caleb took the file his boss offered him and headed out the door. Two minutes later he walked out into the bright sunlight. Feeling like a mole coming out of the ground, he struggled with the urge to turn around and try to change Jim's mind. Instead he walked to his beat-up car and glanced at the calendar on his watch.

So it was May.

The inspection sticker on his car had expired three months ago.

He removed his glasses and rubbed his eyes. The awful truth stared him in the face. He was a human being. He was not a machine. Yet, despite his so-called gifted mind, he couldn't remember the last time he'd smelled roses, taken a nap, eaten decent food and, most damning of all, taken a woman to bed.''

The ponytail would have to go.

Standing beside the table in the bar, Glory mustered a smile as she saw the light of recognition on Caleb's face. He was taller than she remembered, and runner slim with wide shoulders. He still had the same intent, measuring gaze she'd once found unnerving. It was a grown-up man's gaze now, intelligent with a kick of sensual energy, still unnerving. She extended her hand. "Caleb, it's good to see you again."

"Glory Jenkins," he said, clearly surprised. His warm, strong hand captured hers and held it.

"Danson," she corrected softly.

"Married?" He glanced at her left hand.

"Divorced." She slipped her hand from his.

Curiosity flickered through his green eyes, but he simply nodded. "The last time I saw you was in high school." His gaze swept over her. "You look different."

A little of her unease melted away, and she laughed as she sat down. "I hope so. I was all glasses and braces."

"And hair," he added. "You always had long brown hair."

"You didn't," she said pointedly.

"Oh, this," he said, carelessly fingering his short ponytail. "I lose track of time when I'm in the lab sometimes."

"Well, according to the itinerary Dr. Winstead faxed me today, you won't be short on time for any of the trips you'll be taking."

"Not by my choice," he muttered darkly, and lifted a hand to get the attention of the waitress.

Glory waited until they'd ordered drinks. "Am I hearing that you don't want to go on this speaking tour?"

"You are. I belong in the lab. I've never been known for my charm." His lips tilted in a masculine grin. "You should remember that."

Glory sidestepped that land mine. "You were very patient when you tutored me for trigonometry."

"And when you tutored me for English?" he added in a dry, meaningful tone.

"I got the impression you weren't interested in Shakespeare," she hedged, thinking that she liked the deepened tone of his voice.

"So I made sixth-period study hall a living hell for you."

He was goading her, she realized, the same way he had during their junior year when the guidance counselor had come up with the brilliant idea that they should tutor each other. "Is that the way you remember it?" she asked diplomatically.

Caleb chuckled. "You're good. Now tell the truth. How do *you* remember tutoring me?"

"Caleb, it's part of a PR person's job to remain positive about the client."

"Fine. Tell everyone else how brilliant I am, how many degrees I've got and what an all-around damn good guy I am. Tell *me* the truth."

Great. He was as demanding as ever. She shook her head. "Well, I think I've blocked most of it from my mind. But I do remember the term paper."

"That was a horror," he admitted.

"You murdered Shakespeare," she told him. "I spent hours—"

"It felt like centuries," Caleb interjected.

Glory smiled. "At the very least."

They both laughed.

The waitress served their drinks. "You vanished after junior year," she said.

Caleb nodded. "I decided to finish my senior year in summer school. I started college in the fall and went year-round for..." He paused and shrugged. "For centuries. Then I started with Paxton Pharmaceuticals in the research division. It was like coming home." He took a sip of beer and pointed the bottle toward her. "What about you?"

"I graduated from the American University in D.C., worked for a big PR firm for five years, got sidetracked for a while and now I'm starting to pull things back together."

He gazed at her thoughtfully. "You always said you were going to be a politician."

Struggling with a familiar sense of disappointment in herself, Glory looked down at the scarred wooden table. "I married one instead," she said quietly. "But that's a long story with a not-so-happy ending." She took a deep, determined breath and met his gaze straight on. "And we've got plans to make."

Two hours later, Glory had decided the "wild beast" nickname was a misnomer. Wild, maybe. There was something sexually appealing about Caleb, partly that too-smart-to-give-a-damn attitude, partly the way he focused on her while she talked. But he wasn't beastly, she thought with a secret smile as he walked her to her car.

He knocked on the hood of her sedan. "Good, sensible American car."

That nettled her a little. "I wanted a red Porsche."

He raised his eyebrows, and she felt his gaze, this time warming her skin. "Oh, really?" he said in that deep voice, and leaned closer to her.

Her heart pounded fast and hard. Her reaction stunned her into silence. For Pete's sake, she'd only had a diet soda. Why did she feel so giddy?

"I always wondered if your hair was as soft as it looked." He lifted a strand of her hair and skimmed his fingers over it. Her stomach turned a flip.

"Now I know." His gaze, darker and reckless, dipped to her mouth. "I wondered what it would be like to kiss you."

He paused two seconds while Glory tried to gather her wits. Two seconds when she should have done something except stand there as still as stone. Then he lowered his head. He rubbed his warm lips against hers in a sensual exploration that made her feel soft and hot. His tongue teased the seam of her mouth until she opened, and he immediately plunged deeper. She tasted the heady flavor of beer and male need.

He gave a low groan of approval, and the sound bolted through her blood like a shooting star. After living under a constant cloud of criticism and ridicule, she was hungry for a man's approval. Her chest drew into a tight knot, and she might have kissed him for an hour, just to feel this way.

She might have if she hadn't felt the wetness of her tears trailing down her cheeks.

Giving a soft sound of protest, Glory pulled away and turned around, bracing her hands on her dependable sedan. The ground felt as if it was moving. Struggling for breath and sanity, she swiped at her cheeks.

Caleb was looking for a piece of sanity himself. He took a deep breath and shook his head. "I, uh, don't know what to say. It's been a long time."

"For me, too," Glory said in a tight voice.

She looked so vulnerable that he had the strongest urge to pull her into his arms. At the moment he suspected she wouldn't thank him if he did. "I'm sorry if you're upset."

"It's not your fault," she said, half-turning toward him. "My crying. At least, I don't think it is."

Clear as mud, he thought. "I'm not sorry for kissing you," he told her, and saw her stiffen in response. "This isn't going to make a bit of sense to you, but I haven't felt this human in months. If I thought you wouldn't slap me into next week, I'd kiss you again."

Her bottomless blue eyes widened. "Don't," she said quickly, desperately. She bit her lip and managed a little smile. "I'd hate to have to slap a client."

Caleb felt a couple of weird aches, one in his chest, a more familiar one throbbing against his zipper. "So, what should we blame this on?"

Glory shrugged and looked up at the sky. "The moon?"

"The beer," he offered, trying to inject a note of humor.

She laughed, and he nearly wiped his forehead with relief. "Oh, no, it was definitely the diet Coke."

He watched her unlock the car door and slide into the seat. He liked the way she moved, feminine with a controlled energy. Holding the door in his hands, he looked at her again. There was a haunting womanly beauty about her. Life had softened the edges and brought a shadow of pain to her blue eyes. He wondered about the politician husband. He wondered what it would be like to kiss her again. He wondered what it would be like to make love to her.

"It's late," she said. "I need to go. I'll see you in a couple of days." She squared her shoulders. "And Caleb, I'm not drinking any more diet soda when I'm around you."

He laughed. "Right. That's dangerous stuff. Scientifically proven. Take care," he said, and closed the door. Shoving his hands into his pockets, he watched Glory drive her sensible sedan out of the parking lot. She was a beguiling mix. Sedate family car manners with a Ferrari body and a kiss that could charge the deadest engine.

For a few minutes she'd made him forget he was at loose ends. At the same time, he remembered Jim's last bit of ridiculous advice, and Caleb thought he could spend a lot of time wondering what it would be like to make love to Glory, and even more time doing it.

Chapter Two

Glory might have found Caleb's tardiness amusing if she hadn't been so annoyed. She checked her watch, then glanced around the bar and tried to ignore the speculative gaze from the waiter. After sharing that passionate kiss with Caleb, she'd felt embarrassed. Never mind that she'd found it pleasurable, it had been so unprofessional. Where had her mind been?

Since she'd seen Caleb, she had worried that, despite her protest the other night, Caleb might anticipate their relationship as more than business. What if that kiss hadn't been enough? What if he tried to seduce her? What if he decided to focus his formidable single-minded attention on her?

What a joke. He'd canceled three meetings with her. Tonight he was twenty-five minutes late and he hadn't called. Her patience wasn't just waning anymore. It had flown straight out the window.

Hugging the round tray to his chest, the waiter approached her table. "You want to use the phone? I can bring it to the table."

Glory took her keys from her purse and shook her head. "I think this is going to require a personal visit."

The waiter looked skeptical. He had, after all, seen her being stood up four times. He leaned closer. "This is none of my business, but why don't you just dump this guy? He never shows."

Glory gave a long-suffering smile and stood. "He's a client. I can't dump him." *I can just fantasize about dumping him,* she thought as she walked to her car.

Twenty minutes later, as she walked up the sidewalk to Caleb's town house, she recalled her conversation with his boss, Dr. Jim Winstead. She'd explained, as tactfully as she could, her difficulty in gaining Caleb's cooperation.

"Caleb Masters is an extraordinary scientist. When he sets his mind to a goal, he's not easily dissuaded. He's also not easily managed. Since you will be managing him—"

"Me!" she squeaked, and cleared her throat over the thick distress that nearly choked her. *Manage Caleb!* Three months ago her self-esteem had been in such tatters she'd had a tough time making a decision about which shoes to wear. Dr. Winstead might as well ask her to harness a nuclear explosion.

She took a careful, calming breath. "It was my understanding that Caleb and I were to work as a team. I would assist him with his speeches, scheduling, his public relations presence and his interactions with the media.''

A long silence followed. ''It might involve a little more than that.''

Glory waited, and when he didn't explain further, she prompted him. ''Such as?''

''Caleb is very committed to his research. He doesn't want to do this speaking tour,'' Dr Winstead confessed. ''Hell, there's no other way to say it. If you're going to gain his cooperation, you'll have to use bribes, intimidation, brute force, anything.'' He paused a half beat. ''And if you find something that works, let me know what it is.''

With those words echoing in her mind, Glory pressed Caleb's doorbell.

''He might not answer.'' A little boy holding a cat the size of an Alaskan husky walked toward her. He had a hole in one knee of his jeans and a grass stain on the other. His brown hair spiked up in a pronounced cowlick at the crown, and he was quite thin compared to the cat. ''He's been real busy lately,'' he continued. ''When he gets real busy, he don't always hear so good.''

Out of the mouths of babes. Glory rang the doorbell again. ''I'll just keep trying, then. Are you Dr. Masters's neighbor?''

The little boy nodded. ''Next door. He lets me feed Fancy and play with her.''

Confused, Glory did a double take. ''Fancy is his cat?'' She couldn't imagine Caleb owning a pet. He had enough difficulty keeping up with himself.

''Sorta. My mom says we can't have one 'cause I'm only seven and that's not old enough. So, Dr. Caleb told me if I picked out a kitten at the animal shelter and promised to feed it and play with it, we would share custody." He lifted the plump feline toward her. "You can pet her if you want to."

Out of the blue, Glory felt a ripple of tenderness toward Caleb. She rubbed the purring cat and smiled. "It looks like you've been taking very good care of her."

"Yeah." He eyed the door. "My mom says Dr. Caleb's book smart, but he ain't got no common sense." He shrugged. "But I like him. He's—"

"Timmy!" the woman next door called from her doorstep. "Come home. It's time for you to come in now."

"My mom," he said with a sigh. "Gotta go. Wanna hold Fancy?"

"Well, I—"

"Here," he said, dumping the cat in her arms.

Glory stared down in consternation at the still-relaxed animal. The thing weighed a ton. At a loss, she shifted slightly and rang the doorbell.

Three more times.

Caleb finally opened the door. At the sight of him, she nearly forgot she was holding a fifty pound cat. Jeans slung low on his hips, his shirt carelessly unbuttoned at the top with sleeves pushed back on his arms, he leaned against the doorjamb and looked at her with his dark, intent gaze. His mind was clearly on something else, but Glory was certain he'd cataloged everything from her hair to her toes with the slightest extra attention given to the curves that made her body different from his.

A disconcerting warmth suffused her, and she had the sensation of being seen yet not seen at the same time.

He blinked. "Come in. I'm making sure McAllister has backup copies of my files. He's been known to lose things before."

Determined to make up for lost time, Glory stepped through the doorway. "What do I do with your cat?"

He tossed a quick glance over his shoulder and shook his head. "Oh, Fancy. Looks like Timmy's been feeding her too much again. You can put her down anywhere."

Glory began to empathize with the cat. As far as Caleb was concerned, they were both forgotten creatures. She set Fancy down and swallowed her impatience. "We need to—"

"I've been using my modem to transfer some information I found last week," Caleb said as he led the way down the hallway through a sparsely furnished den to a small room crammed full of boxes, electronic equipment and research journals. The battered desk held a pizza delivery box and a state-of-the-art computer. The cursor on the screen blinked with rhythmic insistence.

Glory watched Caleb slide into the chair and pick up the scanner. "It shouldn't take much—" His eyebrows slanted into a frown. "What the—" He grabbed the phone and pushed an automatic dial button. "McAllister, stop screwin' with the modem. I've just got a few more pages—"

Caleb stopped and frowned more deeply. "What do you mean, Dr. Winstead said you shouldn't be receiving anything else from me on-line? This article could make a difference—''

Caleb stood and the room grew smaller, as much from the energy he put off as his height. He scowled, and Glory was glad her name wasn't McAllister. His body was taut with indignation, his mouth drawn in a firm, ominous line, and his eyes glinted with fire. Watching in fascination, she backed toward the doorway. Oddly, she wasn't afraid, she just wanted to give him room.

"Winstead said for you to direct my calls to him. For the next six weeks!'' Caleb's voice rose. "You tell Winstead he can—'' Caleb stopped abruptly, then stared at the telephone receiver. "He hung up,'' he said in an incredulous voice.

A quicksilver memory flashed in her mind of how her ex-husband's silent anger had always chilled her. At first she'd admired his cool self-control in every situation. It wasn't until later, when she'd experienced his ability to freeze her out, that she'd realized his coldheartedness. In contrast, there was something honest and human in Caleb's anger.

"That gutless lab rat hung up on me.''

His gaze finally collided with hers and Glory tried for a reassuring smile. "Sounds like he might have been following orders.''

His gaze darkened and he looked at the phone again. "When I get Winstead—''

Stepping closer, Glory put her hand over his and felt the tension emanating from beneath his skin. "Maybe you'd better get in touch with Dr. Winstead some other time.''

"The article was important.''

She felt a tugging sensation in her chest. Without his research, Caleb was at a loss. His anger was more frustration at being kept out of the lab. Glory understood frustration and loss too well not to empathize. "And your research is very important," she said, following an unbidden instinct to soothe. "That's why we've got to make sure this speaking tour is as effective as it can be."

Caleb's chest expanded as he took a deep breath and visibly reined in his emotions. He turned his gaze on her and regarded her silently. "I forgot about meeting you tonight."

"You're so good for my ego."

His mouth twisting wryly, he turned his large hand around to capture hers. "You've seen my infamous temper now. Think you're going to be able to handle me for six weeks?"

The way Caleb was finally looking at her, giving her his undivided attention, made her stomach dip and sway. Glory hid her doubts with a shrug and pulled her hand away. "No problem," she said in her best PR voice. "But what we need to do now is make plans for this tour."

"I thought the itinerary was already set."

"It is, but we've got to get ready." She counted off the plans on her fingers. "We need to discuss your audience and what your most effective public relations presence will be. Write speeches—"

"Public relations presence?" he repeated skeptically.

"Well, of course," she said, noting that Fancy had entered the room and begun making figure eights around Caleb's legs. She wondered if he noticed.

"Your audiences will range from wealthy conservative types to more liberal activists. Based on those demographics, we'll choose wardrobe to—"

Caleb held up a hand. "Are you telling me you expect me to wear a different suit for every speech?"

"Not every speech. You can use different shirts and ties, but we'll need to bear in mind TV appearances. Some colors look better on camera."

He gave a short laugh. "Do you think I give a rip what tie I'm wearing?"

Impatience stabbed at her, but she tamped it down. "Probably not, but it's my job to help you establish an effective presence."

All careless masculine appeal, Caleb pulled at his shirt, his green eyes gleaming with devilment. With his long hair and day-old beard, he looked rough and ready. "What's not to love?"

Not much, she thought, from a purely feminine point of view. From the PR slant, though, the list was nearly too long to fathom. She stifled a sigh. He was going to be a pain in the rear, but what a sexy pain in the rear. If the difficulty of this assignment was rated one to ten, she'd give it a twenty. Despite that fact, she felt the faintest stirring of challenge she hadn't felt in years. "When was the last time you went shopping?"

He rubbed his unshaven chin thoughtfully. "I bought a steam-cleaned carburetor for my nephew last summer and ordered some stuff from a catalog for Christmas."

She'd save her questions about the steam-cleaned carburetor for later. "The first thing we need to do is get some clothes for you." She glanced at her watch.

"There's a mall close by. If we hurry, we can get it all done in one trip."

Resistance edged across his features and he shook his head. "I need to take care of this article...."

While Caleb gave excuses, Glory recalled Dr. Winstead's words—*bribes, intimidation, brute force.* Mustering her nerve, she stood as tall as her whopping five-foot-five-inch height would allow and pointed her finger at him. "You've canceled three times. You stood me up tonight. You owe me."

He stared down at her for a long moment, then slowly dipped his head. "Okay. What do you want?"

"For the next two hours I want your undivided attention."

With hooded eyes he flicked his gaze over her. "That shouldn't be too difficult."

Glory cursed the swift rush of heat that surged through her. Who did he think he was fooling? The only way she would be able to capture Caleb's attention for any length of time was if she came equipped with test tubes and a keyboard. "We'll see," she murmured, glancing down at Fancy, then back to Caleb before she turned toward the hall. "Don't trip over your cat."

Why didn't Winstead just shoot him? Caleb thought as he followed Glory into a large department store. He considered shopping a waste of time, an annoying task comparable to filing his tax return. He was overdue for that, too. Tonight his clothing selection would be based on comfort and style with an emphasis on quick decisions. He nabbed a salesclerk as soon as they walked into the men's department and made his selections within twenty minutes. He noticed Glory remained silent throughout the whole process, but he caught her returning to one particular tie again and again, stroking her fingers over the crimson silk.

The slow, simple motion of her hands sliding over the fabric drew his attention. While the clerk carried two suits and assorted shirts and ties to the counter, Caleb moved to her side. Her hands looked soft and delicate; her fingernails were painted a light color that said more about grooming than fashion. It was strange, but watching the movement of her fingers made him feel both soothed and restless at the same time. He wondered how it would feel to be explored by her hands.

He caught one of her hands in his. "What color is this?"

She glanced up at him quizzically. "The tie?"

He shook his head. "Your fingernails."

She shrugged. "I call it light pink, but the cosmetic company apparently thought that was bland, so—" She hesitated and looked away as if she were self-conscious.

Curious, Caleb prompted her, "So?"

He felt her sigh drift over his knuckles. "They call it French Kiss," she said in a low voice, and pulled her hand away.

A blistering image stole across his mind. "Damn. I didn't know they could bottle it yet."

Her lips tilted upward in a smile. "Me, either."

Her gaze was nearly concealed by the fringe of her dark lashes, but the impact on his bloodstream was warm and insidious. Caleb narrowed his eyes. He couldn't recall when he'd been this curious about something or someone outside the lab. He pointed to the tie. "You like that one," he said.

"I do,"she admitted, tilting her head to one side to study it. "It's bold, but I like the way the colors contrast."

Caleb went with his gut. "I'll take it."

At the counter Glory pulled out her company charge card at the same time Caleb searched for his checkbook.

She shook her head. "You don't need to do that. I submit the charges, then bill your company. They've already agreed."

Caleb swore under his breath when he found a couple of twenty-dollar bills, but no checkbook or credit cards. "That means my company will be buying ties instead of spending money on research. I'll buy my own clothes."

Glory looked at him in confusion. "But this is part of the budget."

"It shouldn't be." He gestured toward the clerk. "Can you hold this until tomorrow or the next day?"

"Oh, no," Glory said, putting her charge card on the counter. "I'm not taking the chance that you'll forget. We've got five days until we leave for your first speaking engagement."

The clerk reached for the card, but Caleb got it first. "I said I'd pay." He saw the protest forming on her lips. "Why don't you believe me?"

She closed her mouth and paused. He could practically see the wheels turn. "I wouldn't say I don't believe you," she said in a lower voice. "It's just that you have a lot on your mind. You're still transferring information back to the lab, and I don't think picking up the clothes will be a high priority for you."

"Very diplomatic," he said, irritated that she felt she had to handle him with kid gloves. "You don't believe me."

Her eyes flashed and she lifted four fingers. "Four times. We were supposed to meet four times, and you didn't show."

Caleb withstood the criticism. It wasn't the first time he'd heard the same kind of remark. His brother Eli was constantly complaining that he needed to join the real world. Caleb knew he was completely capable of taking care of everyday business. He just didn't consider everyday business all that important.

The reason he hadn't kept the meetings with Glory was partly that he had needed to transfer a mother lode of information to McAllister. The other reason was that Glory was damn distracting, and, out of necessity, Caleb had developed a habit of ruthlessly eliminating anything that drew his attention away from work. During the past few years he had lived a near monklike existence, his focus securely on his research.

With Glory, he didn't feel monklike.

When she walked past him, her feminine scent cranked his testosterone into overdrive. Her straight skirt didn't conceal the inviting curve of her hips. Her blouse draped against the soft swell of her breasts, and he could see the lacy outline of her undergarment beneath it. The suggestion of that lingerie made him want to see more. He wanted to see the pale skin of her chest and abdomen. He wanted to find out if her nipples were sensitive. Caleb believed in using all the senses when he was doing research. With Glory, he wanted to see, he wanted to touch and he wanted to taste.

And she'd probably slap him into the next century if she knew everything he wanted.

He drew in a deep breath of resignation and negotiated. "I'll pick them up tomorrow," he said. Then he added, "On my word."

"Okay," she agreed, her expression reluctant. She checked her watch. "I guess we've got just enough time for phase two."

"Phase two?"

"There's a hair salon in the mall."

Glory window-shopped while Caleb got his hair cut. He wasn't the kind of man who would allow a woman to tell the hairstylist how to cut his hair, just as he hadn't wanted her to select his clothes or drive her car. He had a strong sense of self. She envied him that. She was curious how he'd look after the cut, though, and wondered if he would go so far as to get a buzz.

She relaxed by the fountain, tossing a few coins in for good luck, then admired the well-tended plants. Five minutes before the mall closed she bought two cones of chocolate chip ice cream and met him outside the salon. She blinked when she saw him.

His hair was only an inch shorter, tapered on the sides, with the bangs brushed to the side. The style wasn't conservative; instead it was unconventional, a little rakish, very masculine.

He strode to her side and took one of the ice-cream cones. "Thanks. Like it?"

She looked again. "Umm, I think so. It's not what I expected."

He gave her a knowing glance and gestured toward a short-haired man walking past them. "More like that?"

"Maybe," she admitted, biting back a grin.

"The stylist asked a few questions about my hair-styling routine," he said in a cryptic voice.

Glory smothered a laugh. "And you told her wash, shake and go."

"How did you know?" he asked blandly.

"Lucky guess," she said. "I like it. It's..." She felt his expectant gaze and sensed his curiosity. His expression prompted her to finish, but she was reluctant to use the adjective that came to mind. "I can't think of the right word."

He leaned closer. "Sexy," he said with wry masculine bewilderment. "The hairdresser called it sexy."

The hairdresser was right. Glory felt a buzz on the back of her neck, but didn't comment, instead choosing to concentrate on her melting ice cream. Caleb pulled away and she breathed a sigh of relief.

"Glory Danson! Is that you?"

Her stomach twisted into a knot at the familiar voice, and she braced herself for one of her ex-husband's acquaintances. "Maris, what a surprise."

Maris smiled gamely. "Where have you been? Nobody's seen you since you and Richard—" She hesitated as if she realized her social gaffe. "Well, it's almost as if you dropped off the face of the earth. We've been so worried about you."

Never one to linger over ice cream, Caleb finished his at the same time he saw Glory's face tighten. He didn't spend time trying to read people, but he knew he possessed some capacity for empathy. That was, in fact, part of the reason he avoided people. When he found something wrong, when someone was hurting, his overriding instinct was to fix it. Unfortunately, he'd learned he couldn't fix everything.

At the moment he sensed a rumbling of tension, an underlying pain inside Glory. She was trying to conceal it, but it was there.

He slid his gaze over to Maris and studied her more closely. She was fighting middle age with a conservative though youthful hairstyle and designer clothing, but her jaded eyes and too-shrewd smile gave her away. She emanated the sincerity of an oily politician. He didn't usually waste time judging people, but he didn't like this woman.

Caleb watched a drop of ice cream trickle down Glory's clenched hand. For a moment he wondered if she was going to squash the cone.

"It's nice of you to be concerned," she said in the moderate PR tone he distinguished from her natural husky voice. The PR voice was cool and careful. Caleb liked her natural voice. It reminded him of sunlight. "But I didn't drop anywhere," she continued. "As a matter of fact, I'm working for a PR firm in D.C."

"I'm glad you're keeping busy." Maris turned her inquisitive gaze on Caleb. "And who is your friend?"

What the hell, he thought, and went with his twisted instincts. "Dr. Caleb Masters," he told her, and extended his hand.

"Pleased to meet you," she said with a smile. He could feel her visual reassessment. "I'm Maris

Thorne. You've probably heard of my husband, Senator Robert Thorne.''

Idly noting that several store clerks had pulled down the metal closures, Caleb shrugged. "Can't say that I have.'' He turned his attention back to Glory and lifted her hand to his mouth. "Your ice cream's melting,'' he said, and ran his tongue over the back of her hand.

Her blue eyes huge with shock, Glory gaped at him helplessly.

He heard Maris's soft gasp. "Oh, my.''

Caleb could have done it again, and it would be a long time before he forgot the taste of Glory and chocolate chip ice cream. But Glory was making a strange sound in the back of her throat, and she looked as if she might keel over any minute. The mall lights began to flicker. "Time to take this party home. Good night, Maris,'' he said, then urged Glory toward the mall exit.

"Good night,'' Glory managed to blurt out, and stiffly followed him outside the mall into the darkness.

As soon as they stepped away from the door, everything changed. Caleb could have sworn he heard her snap, crackle and pop as she rounded on him.

"Why on earth did you—'' She shook her head and stared at her hand.

Caleb watched her ice-cream cone tilt to a dangerous angle. "Careful. You might lose your ice cream.''

She looked at him as if he were crazy. "I don't care if I lose my ice cream. What I want to know is what could possibly possess you to, to—'' She took a deep breath. "*Lick* me!''

"It was expedient," Caleb told her.

"Expedient!"

"Your ice cream was melting on your hand and you were talking to Mrs. Politics." When she continued to stare at him in disbelief, he shrugged. "I didn't have a napkin."

"Oh, God," she said, closing her eyes. "Caleb, Maris Thorne will be on the line with this as soon as she can pick up her cellular phone."

"Big mouth, huh?"

She opened her eyes and sighed. "She likes to talk."

"She's one of those self-important political types. Are you going to eat your ice cream?"

Glancing at the melting dessert with little interest, she handed it to him. "Here. Let's go to the car. Maris can be a little egocentric at times," she conceded.

Walking toward the car, Caleb quickly consumed the ice-cream cone. "I didn't like her."

"Well, she's not exactly my best friend." Glory made a face at her sticky fingers.

"Need some more help with your melted ice cream?" Caleb offered.

"No!" Glory immediately said, then fished through her purse. "Give me a minute. I've got a tissue in here somewhere." She pulled one out and rubbed it over her hands.

Caleb stifled the urge to point out that he would have done a better job, and took his keys from his pocket. "Who is?" he asked.

She glanced at him in confusion. "Who is what?"

Watching her under the parking lot lights, he leaned against his car. "Your best friend."

She stopped midmotion and silently stared into space for a long moment, then looked back at him. Her blue eyes were vulnerable, and she bit one side of her lip pensively. "I'm not sure I have one right now," she confessed in a quiet voice.

He heard the hint of longing in her voice, heard it and felt it invade his mind and gut. He identified with the gnawing ache of loneliness easily because he'd spent years denying, *defying* that ache. But when he saw sadness clouding her usually clear blue eyes, all he wanted was to take her in his arms and make her longing go away. All he wanted was to take her mouth and make his own ache go away.

It wouldn't, however, end with a kiss.

The lure was both compelling and dangerous, the choice not as easy as it had been in the past, but, relying on years of practice, Caleb went with the denial and ignored the restless dissatisfaction that rolled through him. Careful not to touch her, he gave a nod and hoped she knew that he understood. Then he opened her car door and motioned her in.

In the darkened den of her rented colonial with her CD player whispering a soothing instrumental collection, Glory rested on her sofa with a cool damp cloth covering her eyes and aching forehead. Her empty wineglass sat on the end table.

Six weeks with Caleb Masters.

Heaven help her, she wasn't sure she could pull it off. The man was completely unpredictable. One moment he was kissing her, the next, standing her up.

And the next moment he was *licking her hand*. "Oh, God," she moaned, still unable to believe it. The gesture had been shocking. It shouldn't have been erotic. The sight of his head bent over her hand, the touch of his tongue on her skin shouldn't have been the least bit arousing. Her heart shouldn't have lunged into her throat, and her skin shouldn't have heated up ten degrees. That's what she'd told herself while she jumped down his throat with both feet.

Just as she'd gathered her equilibrium, he'd blown her out of the water with that casual question about best friends. She could have named a few promising acquaintances she'd made through the Women's Resource Center at the American University, but none were truly best friends.

The reality emphasized her sense of isolation. Glory was working on rebuilding her life, but building friendships took time, and in a metropolitan area like Washington, D.C., time was at a higher premium than money.

She wondered how he'd known to prod into one of her sensitive areas. If she closed her eyes she could still feel the weight of his heavy gaze. He had watched her in his quiet, intense, almost empathetic way. Watched, but didn't touch. And she had felt strangely moved.

Unfortunately, everything he did affected her. It was as if she had an invisible collection of strings, and he knew how to pull them all.

Poor Glory. At another man's mercy.

Absolutely not!

Frustrated, she yanked the washcloth off her forehead and sat up. She wasn't putting up with this anymore. She was damn tired of feeling victimized and out of control, she thought as she stood. She refused to be a wimp.

Flicking on all the lights in the room, she took stock. It was true that her skills were a little rusty, and she could probably use a refresher course in assertiveness training. It was true that Caleb was a nightmare client.

It was also true, however, that she needed to prove herself to her manager. Most of all to herself. With that goal in mind, surely any sexual attraction she felt for Caleb would be the least of her worries.

Chapter Three

Glory tapped her hand against her leg as she waited
outside Caleb's hotel room. It was time to leave for his
first public appearance. He would deliver a speech to
the Chartland, Ohio, Public Forum then join a local
reporter for after-dinner drinks and an interview. Although she refused to give in to an impending sense of
doom, she would have to confess to being a teensy bit
worried about the speech.

Caleb opened his door, tugging at his tie and
swearing. "I knew there was a reason I hadn't worn a
tie in three years." He captured her hand, pulled her
into the room and kicked the door closed behind her.
Even wearing a scowl that matched his black shirt and
pants, he was compelling.

"Let me." Lifting her hands to tie the Windsor
knot, she felt the heat of his chest beneath her fingers

and the weight of his gaze on her. She tried to push aside the sharp coil of tension in her stomach, but she was struck again with the realization that when she thought of Caleb, she always thought of heat.

"You do that like a pro."

Backing away, she shrugged, ironically pleased that her marriage had netted at least one useful skill. "Practice makes perfect. Have you read the speech again?"

He gave a noncommittal half nod. "It's not what I would have written."

She bit her tongue at the urge to point out that he had been *unreachable,* so she'd had to write the speech herself. No need to start an argument before his first appearance. She didn't want to make him nervous, although he didn't appear the least bit anxious—more irritated with the whole thing. "We can work on rewrites later. Right now we need to go. You look terrific, and I'm sure you'll do a great job." Then because she couldn't resist, she added, "Especially since you're so enthusiastic."

He lifted his eyebrow at her last comment as he grabbed a professional journal and the rolled-up sheets that comprised the speech. "Sarcasm?"

Glory shook her head and gave him a wry smile. "Wishful thinking."

They arrived at the auditorium in plenty of time and Glory took a seat in the audience. Overhearing snatches of conversations, she surveyed the group around her and judged them to be receptive, socially conscious people. A good start for Caleb, she thought. By the time the announcer introduced him, the hall was nearly full.

"Good evening," Caleb said. "Thank you for coming tonight. I'm delighted to see so many people who are interested in pharmaceutical research for the treatment of Alzheimer's disease. Over two million people are diagnosed with Alzheimer's. You probably know someone with this disease, or perhaps a member of your family...."

Glory took a deep breath of relief and unclenched her hands. He was following the script. Although she wouldn't accuse him of being effusive, he was sticking with the prepared speech. For the next few minutes he continued reading with a casual, competent ease that seemed to hold everyone's attention. She studied his delivery and approved. He didn't speak too quickly or too slowly. His posture was straight, and he even occasionally glanced at the audience. It could have been much worse. Glory relaxed. Everything was going to be okay.

After the second page of the speech, Caleb stopped speaking and ran his hand through his hair. His face tinged with exasperation, he set the speech aside.

Glory's stomach twisted into a knot.

"Enough of that," Caleb said. "What I'd like to tell you about are some of the emerging drug therapies for Alzheimer's."

Glory gazed helplessly at the sheets of paper on the podium. *He had set the speech aside.*

Caleb loosened his tie. "A major chemicoanatomical change is the degeneration of corticocortical glutamatergic pyramidal neurons..." He lectured the group on the neurological basis for the disease.

It might have been okay if he'd stopped, but like the Energizer bunny with a fresh battery, he went on and on. "Cholinergic axons exercise neurotransmitter effects by..."

After ten minutes she noticed a few people slip out the back. Caleb proceeded to discuss something about neuropathological predilection patterns.

Ten more minutes and the two women beside her wore glazed expressions. The nightmare didn't end until thirty more minutes passed.

The auditorium was nearly empty.

After a full moment of silence, a pitiful smattering of applause sounded. Caleb gathered the papers for the unused speech and muttered, "Thank you." Then he shook hands with the dazed announcer and exited the stage.

Glory felt the nagging onset of a tension headache.

"We've got a half hour until we need to meet the reporter," Glory said as they walked toward the rental car. She needed to block the speech from her mind until they got through the interview. "I have directions to the restaurant. Do you want me to drive?"

He shook his head. "You navigate. I'll drive."

They got into the car and pulled out of the parking lot. "The reporter's name is Jerry Thompson. He's done some articles on science and medicine, but I'm not sure—"

"East or west?" Caleb prompted, pointing at the sign.

Glory reread her directions. "Left at the light, then right at the second light." As Caleb made the appropriate turns, she continued to prepare him for the interview. "I'm not sure what his background is, so he may try to go for the human-interest angle."

"West?" Caleb asked.

She sighed, glancing at the directions again. "I don't do east or west. I do left, right, straight ahead, or turn around you've gone too far."

"Is that a gender distinction?"

For the sake of world peace Glory chose to ignore the remark as she read the last instruction. "The restaurant should be a mile ahead on the left."

He pulled in to the parking lot and stopped, gazing at her silently for a moment. "You haven't said anything about the phenomenal success of my first public appearance."

She searched for something positive. "You obviously know an enormous amount about Alzheimer's disease."

"You're using your PR voice. You do that every time you don't want to be blunt."

She sucked in a deep breath and looked away. "I think we should discuss it after the interview."

Caleb shrugged. "We've got fifteen minutes."

Glory counted to ten. "That's not enough time, and we should—"

"You're angry."

"I'm a little frustrated," she confessed, knowing it was a huge understatement. "But I'll get over it."

"You've shredded that piece of paper."

Glory glanced down at the bits of paper in her hand. "Are you always this persistent?"

"I'm a scientist," he said crisply. "A scientist seeks the truth."

"Okay." She crumpled the pieces of paper into a ball. "The truth is I gave you a perfectly good speech targeted for this particular group. I spent hours preparing it, and you set it aside to deliver a lecture appropriate for someone pursuing a doctorate.''

"Your speech didn't sound like me. It didn't have enough facts, and it was too emotional.''

Glory bit the inside of her cheek to keep from screaming. "Then why didn't you tell me so we could make changes?''

"By the time I read it, I decided you'd be too busy to—''

"Me? Busy!'' That tore it. "I wrote that alone,'' she emphasized, "because pinning you down for a meeting time this week was like trying to nail Jell-O to the wall.''

Caleb gave a long sigh and raked his hand through his hair. "I didn't want to work with you,'' he finally said.

Glory blinked and felt her stomach sink. This was terrible. One of the most important requirements in the client-consultant relationship was maintaining a good rapport. She racked her brain for what she'd done and tried not to give in to an insidious sense of failure. "I don't know what to say. I know we've had some rocky moments, but I didn't realize I'd offended—''

"It's not that,'' Caleb began.

But Glory couldn't seem to stop. She bit her lip. "If it was the clothes—''

"It's not the clothes.''

"The haircut,'' she concluded, feeling a burning sensation behind her eyes. "You didn't want—''

"Stop,'' he told her, his face inches from hers.

Her heart stuttered.

He took her shoulders in his hands. "The only thing about you that offends me is when you use that cool, supercontrolled PR voice. I didn't want to work with you because I can't concentrate worth a damn around you."

Glory swallowed. "Because I talk too much?"

He gave a rough, self-deprecating chuckle. "No. It's because you smell good, and you've got a nice smile. It's because I remember how your hair felt in my hands," he said, sifting his fingers through a strand of her hair. "And how much I liked it." His gaze fell to her lips. "I remember how your mouth felt, and how much I liked it."

Trapped by the power in his green eyes, she stared back, her equilibrium obliterated. She cleared her throat. "Oh," she managed in a weak voice.

"I'm not easily distracted," he told her, rubbing his thumb over her mouth. "It's become a way of life for me to push aside anything that threatens my concentration, but I've been unsuccessful at pushing you aside."

His tone oozed aggravation with his own weakness and a hint, just a hint, of fascination for her. A balm to her shredded ego, the knowledge slipped past her own objections. Glory swallowed. "You sound delighted."

"I'm not," he said bluntly, his finger drifting down her throat. "But there is an expedient way to take care of my distraction."

She wasn't sure she wanted to hear this. He probably wanted her replaced. "And that is?"

"Eliminate the mystery. Settle my curiosity. Answer my questions."

"Questions..."

"I want to make love to you."

Glory's breath froze in her throat. She should have known that was coming. Perhaps she had known it and denied it. She shook her head. "No," she said, pulling back and feeling a jerk when her hair remained in his hand. "We have a professional relationship. It's vital that we—"

"Our professional relationship isn't working very well," he observed. "Every time I'm around you, I think about sex."

A hot image seared her mind. Glory closed her eyes. It was too easy to envision Caleb's nude body pressing against hers, his thighs tangling with hers, his passion driving into her. And because of her broken marriage, she was too vulnerable to his mind-bending attraction for her. "Oh, God, I can't—we can't—" She took a careful breath and whispered, "It's impossible."

Caleb's mouth twisted into a dangerous half grin. "It would be many things, but impossible's not one of them."

Glory gave her aching temples a quick squeeze. "You're not hearing me, Caleb."

"Are you saying you're not attracted to me?"

She should lie; she strongly considered it, but her sense of fairness prevailed. "I didn't say that, but my divorce was final just six months ago, and the whole process wasn't pretty. I'm not where I want to be."

Caleb frowned thoughtfully. "You're still in love with your ex?"

Glory shook her head. "No, but..." She faltered, trying to form the right words. "The relationship damaged me."

He studied her in silence. "Did he abuse you?"

His tone was hard, his face like granite. Glory's chest tightened. The intensity of his gaze made her feel as if she were under a searchlight. "Not physically."

His eyes narrowed and he nodded slowly. "I'm not asking for anything long-term. I can't and I won't. My work is the most important thing in my life, and I've learned that women don't like being second, third or fourth." He sighed. "If I were in the lab, maybe this wouldn't be an issue, but for the next few weeks I'm going to be at loose ends and we're going to be in close company."

Glory bit her lip, then mentioned the unthinkable. "Do you want a different PR consultant?"

Caleb's mouth twisted wryly. "You say that as if there are a dozen people lined up to work with me."

Valid point, she thought. *She* was going to have to keep this situation under control. "Well, then we'll just have to find a way to keep you busy. Since we're visiting these different cities, we ought to be able to come up with something."

"I'm not sleeping well," he told her.

Glory blocked the obvious solution from her mind. "Then we'll have to tire you out a little more during the day."

His gaze drifted over her. "I've got suggestions," he said in a low voice that made her feel warm.

She prayed he wouldn't repeat them to her. "I think we'd better leave this itinerary to me," she said in the firmest tone she could muster. Knowing they really hadn't settled anything, she glanced at her watch and cleared her throat. "It's about time to meet the press. Your first interview."

His expression said she wasn't getting away with anything. His eyes promised *later,* but he pushed open his car door. "I can't wait."

Twenty minutes later Glory feared the interview was going to turn out the same as Caleb's speech. He kept calling the reporter Gary. The man's name was Jerry. Caleb's answers also sounded like a textbook, abounding in three-dollar scientific terms.

She had to give the reporter credit. He tried to keep up, for a while, anyway, his pleasant round face crinkled with confusion, then suspicion.

He tapped his pad with his pencil. "I've got one more question," Jerry said. "Are you deliberately talking over my head to put me off or because you don't care what kind of article I write?"

Caleb stopped. He gave Jerry a look of grudging regard. "You're astute for a reporter."

"You're dumb for a genius," Jerry returned.

Alarm shot through Glory. She watched Caleb closely, ready to defend him, but he didn't verbally rip the reporter to shreds. Instead Caleb chuckled, then sobered. "It's easier to talk about the scientific basis for the disease and the research process than the everyday reality of AD. The everyday reality of AD is painful and desperate."

"When you think about it, how does that everyday reality affect you as a researcher?"

Caleb glanced down at the table. "It makes me want to hurry. It means," he said in a voice low but full of power, "there's no time to waste."

Jerry was quiet for a moment. "I think we've got our story."

Glory's heart twisted. Jerry would get his story, and Caleb, she sensed, would lie awake tonight cursing every moment that passed that he wasn't in the lab.

Caleb dragged himself out of bed the next morning when the knocking at his door didn't stop. Tugging on his jeans, he grumbled, "I'm coming. I'm coming."

He opened the door to Glory. Through his bleary-eyed gaze she looked fresh, feminine and disgustingly alert. In contrast, he felt like the dregs of day-old coffee. "Hi," he managed in a gruff voice.

"Hi," she returned softly. Carrying a tray of fruit, pastries, orange juice and coffee, she gazed at his bare chest then glanced away. "Sorry I woke you. It's after ten, and I thought I'd better make sure you were still alive."

"Yeah, I swam a few laps in the hotel pool after we got back last night." He covered a yawn with his hand and followed her to the small table on the other side of the room.

"That was pretty late," she said with a small frown of concern as she set the food on the table. "I didn't know the pool was still open."

"It wasn't. I bribed the front desk clerk." Caleb tried to recall the last time someone besides a waitress had served him breakfast, and came up empty. Her thoughtfulness defused his irritation. "What did I do to get room service from Glory?"

"Well, I thought the interview last night was tough," she began, and pulled out the newspaper she'd tucked under her arm.

Caleb agreed. He hadn't expected to spill his guts to some reporter he'd never met before in his life. God, he dreaded the article.

"I remembered what you said about having difficulty sleeping, and I was, well..." She met his gaze. "I was concerned about you."

He blinked. When had anyone worried about him? A warm sensation spread through his gut. He looked at Glory, and wondered again what he was missing because of the life he had chosen.

She soothed and aroused him. Her voice drifted gently over his ragged nerve endings. Her scent lured, her smile offered friendship and her eyes, alternately flashing honesty and feminine secrets, seduced him.

Her gaze slipped over his bare chest again. He wondered how her hands would feel on his skin. This time she cleared her throat when she looked away. "They ran the piece on you this morning, front page of section C."

He sat in the chair and flicked his gaze over the paper. "Modern Day Knight Of The Round Table," he repeated, stunned by the headline. He quickly scanned the article, which put an emphasis on Caleb's drive to find a drug for AD. Rubbing a hand over his eyes, he shook his head. "Next they'll be calling me a superhero."

"It's great," Glory said. "He captured the best of you and put it in print for all of Chartland to see."

He slid a glance at her. "You don't actually believe this, do you?"

"Absolutely," she said, her eyes clear and honest. "You're single-minded to the point of driving everyone around you crazy, but it's not because you're some self-absorbed scientist. It's because you really care about what you do."

He grimaced at the sensation of being emotionally buck naked before the rest of the world. He didn't like it. "So, in your expert opinion, this is good," he said, and took a bite of croissant.

"Not good. Great," she told him. "I'm getting calls for you to do more interviews. Better yet, the local affiliate for a national television network wants you on the noon show."

The bread caught in his throat. "Not TV."

Her expression commiserating, she nodded. "Yes. TV." She held up her hand when he opened his mouth. "But remember that since it's TV, your interview probably won't last more than five minutes. Ten minutes, tops."

"And you want me to bare my innermost thoughts to some stranger on television," he concluded. The thought turned his stomach.

Glory bit her lip and sat beside him. She touched his hand. "If you really, really don't want to, you don't have to. I can call the station and turn them down."

It was on the tip of his tongue to say, "Do it." Caleb had always been extremely private. The fact that she wasn't forcing him, however, gave him pause. "I hear a but."

"This is a terrific opportunity for you to tell people what you want them to know about what you're doing."

"Are you saying the TV reporter won't try to get into all that emotional BS with me?"

"No," she said reluctantly. "But what you've got to remember about interviews is that you don't necessarily have to answer the question you're asked."

Caleb groaned, but he didn't move his hand, because he liked the way her fingers felt on his. He resisted the urge to clasp his hand around hers and bring her hand to his chest. "Sounds like PR BS to me."

Her eyes met his, bold, direct and sexy. Her smile lifted in a tantalizing grin that generated a gnawing ache inside him. "That's because it is."

He was a tease.

Glory watched Caleb with the young woman reporter as he sort of answered some of her questions and sidestepped others. He wasn't hostile about it, but he was clearly determined to keep things under control. He gave just enough to make the audience curious, just enough to make them want more.

Battling the sting of her own curiosity, Glory shook her head. She wondered if he had a clue about his appeal. At the end of his segment she noticed that the woman reporter asked him more questions after the camera stopped running, then gave him her business card.

He looked up and found Glory with his green gaze. She saw the wry but sexy "How'd I do?" look on his face and smiled.

As he strode toward her, she pushed aside her confusing mix of emotions. After Caleb's spiel about how he could not get involved in a long-term relationship, it should have been easy to focus on keeping their businesslike rapport. Glory found, however, she was feeling more instead of less. Something had happened inside her when she'd watched Caleb's honesty during that grueling interview last night. He would probably laugh her off the block if she said it, but Glory felt a strange sort of connection with him. "Okay?" she asked when he stood in front of her.

"Yeah."

"You had that reporter wrapped around your finger."

He shrugged. "She mentioned something about dinner."

Glory felt her stomach dip. "Did you want to go?"

"Don't I have another public appearance tonight?"

"Yes, but—" Glory tamped down her own feelings and took a deep breath. "We can work something out with your schedule if you'd like to see her. She is attractive," Glory conceded.

"I hadn't noticed," Caleb said, his gaze meshing with hers. When she didn't say anything else, he lifted an eyebrow, making his preference clear. "I thought we were having dinner together."

Her heart squeezed in her chest. "We are, but I—" Glory stopped, suddenly feeling foolish about impulsively accepting his invitation.

"Another but," Caleb muttered, and loosened his tie. "Let's get out of here."

Glory quickly thanked the producer and followed Caleb out of the small station. He was nearly to the car before she caught up with him. "I kind of thought of something we could do this afternoon."

He paused and looked at her. Sensing he could read the uneasiness in her eyes, she wished for a pair of sunglasses.

"Kind of thought of something," he repeated.

Glory sighed in disgust at her inarticulate explanation. For heaven's sake, she was paid to be articulate. "I thought about what you said about not sleeping and how you probably feel at loose ends since you're not in the lab and I decided you might enjoy doing something new and totally different."

"Uh-huh," he said, not helping her one bit. "Such as?"

"Such as go-cart racing," she said doubtfully.

He stared at her in surprise for a long moment. "Okay," he said in a solemn voice that didn't match the glint in his eyes. "Something new and totally different."

His agreeable response caught her off guard. "If you would rather do—"

"You'll be racing, too," he said, and he slowly grinned.

"If you like." Glory looked at his white teeth and wondered what she'd gotten herself into.

"By all means." He opened her car door. "But just to make it interesting, let's place a small wager."

"Wager," she repeated warily as she got into the car.

"A little bet between the novice and the pro," Caleb explained in a patient voice. "Don't worry. It won't cost you a penny."

For some reason Glory wasn't worried about her pennies.

After lunch they took several spins around the racetrack. Glory had given him a run for his money during the first two races, but he'd left her eating his dust on the rest of them. While rounding one of her last curves, she'd turned her head in an awkward position and her neck felt slightly strained. Glory absently rubbed at it and watched Caleb. He looked exhilarated, triumphant and just a little guilty.

She pulled off her helmet and shot him a glance of mock disgust. "You could have warned me. I thought I was widening your horizons, providing some balance for your deprived life."

He tugged off his own helmet and handed it to the ride operator. "It's been years," he confessed. "My younger brother, Ash, used to bug me to take him to the go-cart rides. I got bored standing around watching, so I had to race him. And win," he added with a twist of his lips. "Middle child syndrome."

"I forgot about Ash," she said, dimly recalling Caleb's younger brother as they walked away from the track. "What's he doing now?"

"Laying brick," Caleb said, shaking his head as if the notion amused him. "He just moved to Raleigh where my older brother, Eli, lives. Eli's got a son. He's a neat kid."

She saw a hint of warm affection in Caleb's eyes. "Do you see them much?"

He shrugged. "I get down there every once in a while, but work keeps me busy. A couple of times I forgot to show and Eli blessed me out." He shook his head. "Sometimes I wonder if he and Winstead are involved in some sort of conspiracy to change me. They both say nearly the same things."

"Such as?"

Caleb hesitated and narrowed his eyes. "Such as I need to *get a life* outside the lab."

Sensing his frustration, Glory nodded. "And you don't agree?"

"My life *is* the lab," Caleb said in a crisp voice. "But according to Dr. Winstead, my way isn't working. So it looks like I'll have to make some changes anyway."

It was difficult for Glory to comprehend devoting your entire life to one cause. The only time she'd done it had been with her marriage, and that had been a huge mistake. "Would it be so difficult to get involved in a few extracurricular activities?"

"I don't know. I've never done it before. I don't know how to give only a fraction of myself to research. It's always been all or nothing with me."

For a moment Glory was quiet, and the only sound was their feet against the gravel in the parking lot. The conversation had gotten entirely too heavy, and she felt a driving need to help Caleb lighten up. She gave a dramatic sigh. "Well, that certainly explains Fancy's weight."

Caleb did a double take. "Fancy!" he said, perplexed.

Glory nodded soberly. "Oh, yes. She overeats because she's suffering from emotional deprivation." She lowered her voice. "You really shouldn't ignore her."

Caleb stared at her in disbelief. "You're crazy. That cat weighs a ton because Timmy overfeeds her."

Glory bit her lip to keep from smiling and continued walking. "I wouldn't be too sure about that. Think of the research about the relationship between weight gain and depression."

"That's for humans," he told her.

"But can you be sure?" Glory asked in the most dismal tone she could muster considering she was about to burst a rib to keep from laughing.

Caleb snagged her shoulder and urged her back around. "Do you really believe this?"

Glory paused and met his gaze. "About as much as I should have believed you when you wanted to place a small wager between the novice and the pro. You still haven't told me what the stakes were."

When she saw his expression shift in comprehension as he shook his head in indulgent masculine reproach, Glory ignored the way her heart fluttered in her chest. She denied the stab of feminine uneasiness as he stepped closer.

"Gotcha, smarty-pants," she whispered, her breath inexplicably scarce.

Caleb trailed his finger down her jaw at the same time his gaze swept across her mouth. Sexual retribution darkened his eyes. "We'll see."

Chapter Four

Caleb's speech was at best an awkward marriage between her version and his. He read the first three and a half pages of her speech, then in midparagraph he launched into a brief description of what his lab was trying to accomplish.

Glory rubbed her stiff neck as she assessed his presentation. It definitely needed work. Tonight, however, he kept his discourse brief enough that most of the audience remained awake and in their seats. At the end he switched back to the last few paragraphs of her speech.

Not great, she thought. Not even good. But better than last night.

She was still wondering what he had in mind for the silly bet they'd made with the go-carts. Every time she'd asked him about it during dinner, he'd brushed off her concern and told her not to worry, but the intent way he gazed at her worried her greatly.

It must have something to do with her lukewarm sexual experience in her marriage, but frankly, Glory had never understood what all the fuss was about. Something about Caleb, however, made her wonder if she'd missed out on something. It was crazy, but Caleb made her aware of her femininity in a way she'd never been before.

Glory tried to brush her crazy thoughts aside as Caleb conducted a mini-interview with a reporter right after his speech, then joined her to head back to the hotel. "Any more reporters?" he asked as they walked toward their rooms.

"There's a possibility for a telephone interview after we get back to Washington," Glory said, stretching her neck and wincing.

"No more TV appearances," he continued, watching her rub her neck.

"Not during this trip."

"And no more go-carts tonight?" he asked, reluctant to leave her.

She shook her head and winced again as they stopped outside her room. "Not for me. I must have turned my head the wrong way. My neck is killing me."

Seeing her pull out her room key card, Caleb took it from her hand and opened her door. "Let me see if—"

Glory gave a stiff shake of her head. "You don't need—"

"I'm calling in the bet on the go-carts." In no mood for a protest, Caleb urged her through the door.

"Now?"

"Now." He flicked on the bathroom light, but left the others off. Then he put a chair in front of her.

When she just stood there looking at him, he said, "Sit."

She did, reluctantly. "I don't know what you're planning or why, but it's not necessary. If I get a good night's rest, I'm sure I'll feel better in the morning."

Caleb ignored her. She was using the PR voice again. "Close your eyes." He put his hand on her right shoulder.

"I really—"

With his other hand he unzipped the top three inches of her dress.

Glory gasped. "What are you doing? What—"

Caleb began to knead her shoulder and she moaned. "You're in good hands," he promised, keeping his voice low. "I'm an expert on stiff necks." He moved his fingers slightly up her neck. "Is this where it hurts?"

Glory bit her lip. "Up a little."

Caleb made the adjustment and she moaned again. The feminine sound reverberated inside him. For the next few moments they said nothing, and Caleb became acutely aware of the silky warmth of her skin and her hair drifting over his hand.

He lifted her hair off her neck and her scent filled his nostrils. Her eyes were closed, her lips slightly parted. Arousal stirred within him. She would wear the same expression if he was making love to her. Drawing in a deep breath, he was struck with the thought that touching the back of Glory's neck was an intimate act.

He watched her face and felt her faint sigh when she began to relax. For the moment, she trusted him. She knew he was trying to help her feel better. The knowledge gave him a deep sense of satisfaction.

"You have a little knot," he murmured, feeling the tiny nodule beneath his fingers. "Right here."

"Yesss," she whispered, and Caleb's body reacted to all the sexual implications of that little word.

As he continued the gentle massage with one hand, he lightly traced the straight line of her spine with his forefinger until the zipper stopped him. She gave a little shiver, and even in the muted light from the bathroom he could see the goose bumps on her skin. He grinned and did it again. "Tickle?"

"A little," she admitted.

"But you like it."

"I guess." Her confession was low and reluctant.

"What else do you like?" He slipped his hand around and explored the delicate bones encircling her throat.

Glory inhaled a careful breath. She felt warm, almost drugged. "I, uh—" She cleared her throat. "I don't know."

He shifted his fingers. "I can feel your pulse right here." He paused a moment. "It's fast."

Self-consciousness encroached on her sense of well-being and she almost protested. Then, with the lightest of touches, he slid his fingertips up her throat to her chin. And her desire to stop him died in her throat. Glory never would have dreamed Caleb would have such sensitive hands. He continued the feather-light exploration over her cheeks and eyelids, then across her brow.

The soft darkness covered them like a blanket. With his warmth at her back she was relaxed, yet sensitized to his every touch. A second passed, and his finger traced the seam of her lips, back and forth. Warmth suffused her, and she sighed.

"You're so soft," he murmured, and he pulled gently on her bottom lip.

Glory instinctively opened her mouth and Caleb touched her tongue. In that instant everything changed. The pad of his finger, the salty taste of his skin, was invasive and erotic.

Her heart hammered against her ribs. Anticipation tightened her throat. Her breasts swelled against the lace of her bra. Her instincts took over again and she curled her tongue around his fingertip and suckled.

Dimly she heard Caleb's swift indrawn breath. He stopped the mesmerizing massage on her neck and skimmed his hand around to her chest. Glory couldn't breathe.

Slowly he smoothed his hand toward her breasts.

She waited, her stomach twisting in arousal until he slid his fingertips beneath the cups of her bra and brushed her erect nipples.

They both groaned.

Caleb pulled his hand from her mouth and held her from behind, bowing his head against hers. His fingers spread wide, he caressed and explored her breasts. "You like that?" he asked in a rough voice.

Unable to push one single word past her tight throat, Glory bit her lip and nodded.

"I want to push this zipper the rest of the way down, ditch this dress and look my fill," he told her in a tone that was as quiet and soothing as his hands had been just moments before. The words, however, were anything but soothing, and underneath the surface she felt the concealed vibration of his need humming through her. His mouth nuzzled just behind her ear. "Then I want to put my mouth where my hand is."

Glory closed her eyes. The image made her ache.

"I want to touch your whole body like I've touched your neck and face. Then I want to find out what you feel like on the inside."

Glory turned to liquid.

"Do you know what I'm saying?"

"Yes," she whispered, shaken by the strength of her arousal.

"You're soft and sweet, Glory." He rubbed his cheek against her hair. "And I'm hard."

Her heart twisted. She heard the basic male need in his voice. Caught between denial and sharp desire that had taken her by surprise, she stiffened. A thread of apprehension shot through her. Her face felt hot as fire. *She couldn't. She shouldn't.*

"There's a lot I want to do with you," he muttered, easing his splayed hand away from her breasts. As if he'd sensed her moment of doubt, he pulled back. His sigh was full of resignation. "But not tonight."

She felt him scoop her hair off her neck, then his smooth, hard mouth warmed the bare, vulnerable nape of her neck before he stood straight. She heard him take another deep breath. "Better?" he asked.

Her insides were in a riot. *Better?* She swallowed and turned to look at him. "What?"

The darkness shadowed his face, but his tension throbbed between them. "Your neck. Is it better?"

At the moment her neck was the least of her concerns. "Yes," she managed to say. "Thank—"

The slice of his hand in the air cut her off. "Good. I'll see you tomorrow."

He left before she could gather herself and do something or say something, God knew what. *Thank you for making my neck feel better and turning my body into a mass of quivering hormones.*

Glory closed her eyes and wrapped her arms over her still-swollen breasts. Why had he stopped? she wondered. The galling truth was that she probably would have let him continue despite her fleeting panic. In the darkness his low voice, his gentle touch, his surprising sensitivity had somehow made everything okay.

So, why had he stopped? She knew why he'd started. She could almost hear his explanation. "It was expedient. Your neck was hurting. I knew how to fix it."

One thing for sure, after tonight she had a much better understanding of what all the fuss was about.

Glory ducked her head and moaned. This was tougher than she'd thought it would be. Caleb was more complex than she'd counted on. He was different from the brilliant but weird kid she'd known in high school, more than a man with a mission. She couldn't get past his tenderness. Her mind whirled and her heart pumped as if he were still in the room. She took a deep breath.

But it didn't help. His scent clung to the air. She still couldn't get past his tenderness, and with a vague sense of foreboding she wondered if she ever would.

* * *

Caleb slapped his hotel room key card down on the dresser and swore. He jerked off his tie and plowed his hand through his hair in agitation.

His body vibrating with unspent sexual energy, he was so hot and hard he was shaking with it. He stared at his trembling hand and swore again. This was the price he had to pay for becoming human again, for joining the human race. Caleb didn't like it one bit.

In the darkness of his room he drew in a deep breath and moved toward the window. He didn't make a habit of evaluating himself. As far as he was concerned, it was a monstrous waste of time and boring as hell.

Some moments, however, demanded self-reflection. While his body tortured him for his restraint with Glory, he stared out at the city lights and knew he had good reason for the choices he made. It was easier to focus on work and distance himself from the people around him. When he allowed himself to relate to people, Caleb sensed the pain and saw the need. The next step was caring. The next, a relationship, and unfortunately, he'd never learned how to balance relationships and research.

The combination appeared impossible to him.

He didn't need relationships. He didn't need anyone, let alone a woman, taking up space in his mind.

The image of Glory, still and waiting beneath his hands, mocked him. His hands clenched at the remembered texture of her skin.

It was just sex, he told himself. He needed to take her, to explore every inch of her body, to sink so deep inside her that, for at least a moment, he could forget all about research and racing the ticking clock against a ravaging disease.

There was more than his unslaked lust to consider, he thought as he pressed his heated forehead against the cool glass. For all her political correctness, Glory was a beguiling mix of need and generosity, strength and vulnerability. She wasn't hard and she wasn't tough. His brother Ash would call her a high maintenance woman.

Not a great choice for a quick affair, Caleb thought wryly, but he didn't see any other options. Glory was the woman who intruded on his thoughts and kept him from sleep, yet her vulnerability gave him pause. Before he made love to her, he would have to make sure she was strong enough to walk away from him when he went back to the lab and didn't give her the attention she needed and deserved.

The thought pinched, and Caleb laughed shortly without humor. Who was he kidding? The life and work he'd chosen would never allow him to experience the usual relationships most men did, such as marriage and children. Glory might have let down her guard tonight. She might even be susceptible to him. But she knew what kind of man he was.

He would be lucky if he got one night of Glory Danson. Just one night.

Caleb scribbled an elaborate chemical equation on a scrap of paper during the one-hour return flight to Washington. Glory was acting so carefully polite it made his teeth hurt. He felt her uneasy, surreptitious gaze for the fifth time in the same number of minutes and his patience snapped.

"Let's get this over with," he muttered, not meeting her gaze because she'd blushed every time he'd barely looked at her this morning. He kept his voice at a level intended for her ears only. "Your neck hurt, and I rubbed it. I wanted to touch you more, so I did. Your face, your throat, your breasts. I liked it and you did, too. I stopped, so there's no—"

"Why?" she asked.

His gut twisted at the softness of her voice, and he turned to stare at her. "You didn't want me to stop?"

Uncertainty flashed in her eyes. Her cheeks bloomed again, but this time Caleb didn't look away.

She cleared her throat. "No. We, uh, needed for you to stop. Things had gotten out of hand. It was best for you to stop," she continued emphatically as if she'd had this same conversation with herself. "I guess I was just curious...." Shrugging, she gave an exasperated sigh. "Forget it. It doesn't really matter."

She was trying for a semblance of cool control and not quite making it. Caleb liked her better because of it. "I stopped because you weren't sure you wanted to go on. I could tell by the way your breath changed and your body stiffened." When she just looked at him in surprise, he felt compelled to make himself clear. "I'm not going to take anything you don't want to give. That's not the way I want you."

Glory swallowed, but still didn't say anything.

Caleb dipped his head closer to hers. "Am I getting through?"

She took a measured breath and looked away. "Your bluntness is a little disconcerting."

"I could be more blunt," he told her.

"That's not necessary," she said quickly, and glanced at the empty seat beside her.

"I don't want any confusion. I want you, but you're going to name the time."

"Caleb—"

He sighed. "I don't want you uncomfortable because of what happened last night."

Glory looked up as if she were seeking help. "Must we discuss this now?"

"You want to talk about it a different time?"

"No," she nearly wailed, then struggled to compose herself. "I don't think it would be wise for us to—to—"

"Have sex."

She shot him a warning glance. "Right."

"I didn't say it would be wise. Just expedient," he said, taking in her wide eyes and high color. "Just necessary."

She bit her lip and shook her head. "We don't share the same philosophy in this area, Caleb."

"Possibly," he conceded. "But I don't want you blushing every time you think about the fact that I touched your breasts."

Her eyes flashed. "Well, maybe you can't control it, and maybe I can't control it, either."

Caleb paused. She had nailed the entire situation without intending to. His thoughts about Glory were out of control. "Agreed," he murmured, and turned back to his chemical equation. This he could control.

During the rest of the flight they didn't speak much. Caleb scribbled something illegible on a piece of paper while Glory tried to write a press release. Of its own volition, her gaze kept sliding over to Caleb. She couldn't help wondering what was going on in that brilliant mind of his. Sensitive one moment, blunt the next, he confused the dickens out of her. How could a man with such a callous, superficial attitude toward sex have been so attuned to her last night?

It had probably just been an aberration, she thought as the plane began its descent. A crazy, one-time, never-to-be-repeated experience.

Like a lightning bolt.

Glory didn't like the comparison. If lightning didn't kill, it left a nasty burn.

Pushing the thought from her mind, she concentrated on gathering her belongings. Caleb was so focused on his notes that he didn't seem to notice when they landed. Glory gave him a gentle nudge and made her way to the luggage ramp. She felt Caleb at her back as they waited.

"We need to work on your speech," she said to break the tension between them. "We can meet at a restaurant or I can come to your house."

"Let's try your place this time," he said, surprising her. "There are too many distractions at my house."

"Okay," she said, feeling oddly reluctant. She glanced at him and felt as if he'd invaded her space again. Her home was her haven. Since her divorce, she endured a lengthy commute to her rented home in Sykesville, Maryland, because she wanted to get away from the rushed, power-hungry atmosphere that permeated the city. "You probably want to take a breather from all this. How about Tuesday night?" That should give her enough time to regain her equilibrium.

He shrugged. "Tuesday's fine." He pointed to the conveyor belt. "That one yours?"

Glory nodded and reached for it at the same time he did. "Yes, but I—"

Caleb picked up her suitcase, then grabbed his own and headed toward the exit.

"I can carry my own bag," she told him, inexplicably uncomfortable with the courtesy. After the intimacy of last night, she wanted to draw a big black line between them.

His mouth quirked. "So can I."

"But you don't—"

"It's heavy," he told her, shoving open the glass door. The midday heat and humidity hit them with force. "And I'm stronger."

That statement should have sounded insufferably macho, but Caleb made it sound practical. He gestured for a taxi.

"Are you always this logical?"

He glanced down at her, his gaze assessing. "Unfortunately, everything doesn't follow the rules of logic."

He meant her, of course.

The taxi beeped and pulled up to the curb. "Here's your cab," he said, and pulled open the door.

Glory resisted. "You take it. You're the client," she responded, taking the opportunity to draw that black line between them again.

He wrinkled his face in frustration. "Yeah," he conceded. "But you're the woman."

Glory blinked. "Manners?" she exclaimed before she could stop herself, then covered her mouth before anything else popped out.

Caleb scowled. "My father drilled us. Said he wanted us to be gentlemen. God, what a nag he was," he grumbled. "Most of it didn't stick, but it comes out every now and then when I least expect it." He handed her suitcase to the driver and turned back to her, his mouth twisting in a mocking grin that held entirely too much appeal. "It should keep you on your toes."

Fighting an unwelcome tug toward him, she just shook her head. If she stood on her toes much longer, she was going to end up with a cramp.

Glory stood in the drizzle outside her car and stared at the oak tree that looked like a giant splinter sticking out of the roof of her home. Her stomach sank to her knees.

Dampness seeped into her white blouse, but she didn't move, reluctant to face what waited inside. Two doors down, a family was carrying out boxes and a crib. Although it wasn't sundown yet, it was dark enough for lights. Unfortunately, it appeared the electricity was out. Across the street a man sat in a minivan with his children, a cellular phone pressed to his ear. A sure sign the phones were out, too.

Glory sighed. While she'd been putting together press kits in the relative safety of her downtown office building, a thunderstorm had rocked through the area. As she'd driven closer to her neighborhood, she'd heard radio reports of damaged homes. The term *uninhabitable* had been used repeatedly to describe several houses. She just hadn't realized her house would be one of them.

Pushing a damp lock of hair behind her ear, she trudged up the front steps and opened her door. The foyer looked untouched, but the wind whistled eerily. Glory grimaced. She didn't get far up her steps before she saw the demolished ceiling of her second-story hallway and the drenched carpet littered with leaves and branches. Hurrying the rest of the way to her bedroom, Glory told herself not to get upset when she saw her crushed bed littered with roof tiles. The roof could be repaired, the bed and carpet replaced.

She told herself it was just an unfortunate inconvenience, but underneath it all, it meant more. Although she rented the house, she'd chosen it carefully. It had been one of the steps she'd taken to rebuilding her identity after the divorce, and to see the house nearly destroyed shook her.

Within five minutes she'd numbly assessed the damage and was in her car placing a call on her own cellular phone to the real-estate agent. The only saving grace to this evening, she thought, was that Caleb would probably forget they were supposed to meet tonight to nail down a speech.

"The tree is in two of the bedrooms upstairs," she told the rental agent, and pushed back an encroaching sense of distress. "There's glass all over the ground floor. The wind must have shattered the windows."

The agent mentioned something about needing to contact the owner before making any major repairs.

Frustration welled inside Glory. "I'm not sure you understand. My bedroom is wrecked. It's still raining, so everything inside that house is just going to get wetter and wetter unless somebody at least covers up that hole in the roof."

The agent repeated herself, then suggested that Glory make arrangements to stay with friends or family for the next few days.

Glory didn't bother to inform the woman that she had no family in the area and that most of her so-called friends had abandoned her after her divorce. Fighting opposing urges to cry or lash out, she said goodbye, hung up and stared at the phone.

That was how Caleb found her.

Her hair hung damply to her shoulders and her head was tilted at a dejected angle. Clearly surrendering to a private moment of misery, Glory wasn't even aware of his presence. He heard her soft sigh and was blind-sided with such an overwhelming urge to take her in his arms that he shoved his hands into his pockets to prevent it.

He cleared his throat.

She jerked her head up and stared at him.

Caleb took in another effect of the rain. Her blouse was transparent and her nipples looked like berries through the prettiest bit of lace he'd ever seen in his life. Torn between the desire to touch her and an urge to cover her, Caleb fixed his gaze on her unhappy eyes.

"Straight line winds," he said. Factual information about what had caused the destruction was the only comfort he could offer.

She blinked. "What?"

He waved his hand. "The meteorologist said the storm brought straight line winds up to eighty miles per hour."

"I wondered if it was a tornado," she said in a distracted voice. "The inside of the house..." She shrugged as if words weren't adequate.

"You need to get anything out of there?"

She looked uncertain. "Uh, some clothes I guess." She started to get out of the car and Caleb shot out a hand to steady her when she stumbled.

"Thanks," she murmured. "I guess I need to get a toothbrush and—"

He watched her wobble and put both hands on her shoulders to stop her. "Tell me what you want and I'll get it for you."

Glory shook her head. "No. It'll just take a—"

Caleb gently squeezed her shoulders to get her attention. "You look like you're going to fall on your face."

Her gaze trailed away from his, but she made a visible effort to stiffen her spine. "I'm not."

"Sit in the car."

She glared at him, her eyes flashing. "You know, you really ought to consider taking an assertiveness training course. There are moments when your behavior is beyond aggressive." She shook her head in irritation. "Besides, you'll never remember it all. I need suits for work, jeans and T-shirts, and my nightshirt. I need my makeup and my curling iron. I need underwear," she said as if she thought that would put him off.

"Which room?" he asked blandly as he shoved her back toward the car.

"This is ridiculous," she muttered. "I can—"

"Yeah, you could do this if I weren't here. But I am, so you don't need to." He met her blue-eyed gaze and let that sink in for a moment, then went on. "Toothbrush, suits, jeans, T-shirts, nightshirt, makeup, curling iron and underwear. You need another pair of shoes, too. Which room?'' he persisted.

Her face shadowed with reluctance and weariness, she sighed and crossed her arms over her chest. ''Second floor, last door on the left. Watch the glass.''

Caleb was already moving toward the house. In her bedroom he stepped past branches and ceiling tiles to collect everything. This was going to be one hell of a mess to clean up, he thought.

He opened a half-dozen drawers before he found her lingerie. The sight of all that satin and lace stopped him like a fire alarm. An image of Glory barely concealed in the revealing fabric made his blood heat. Ever since that night in the dark when he'd touched her, his imagination had taunted him with what he'd felt but hadn't seen. Swearing, he sank his fingers into a handful of panties, grabbed one bra, then another just because the black garment aroused . . . his curiosity.

He had left her bedroom and was just about to open the front door when he heard a sound in another downstairs room. Following the faint noise, he found Glory in her den pulling a picture off the wall. ''You were planning on wearing that tomorrow?''

Her cheeks colored with embarrassment, she glanced up and shook her head. ''I picked it out a few months ago, and I guess it has sentimental value.'' She held the picture protectively against her chest. ''I don't think anyone would take it, but I don't want to leave it.''

That was good enough for Caleb. He would take a closer look at the picture later. ''Okay,'' he replied, and tried to think of anything else a woman might consider important. "Jewelry?"

"No, I sold all of it to buy the car," she said, the temperature of her voice dropping thirty degrees. "The earrings I'm wearing and my watch will do."

His opinion of her ex sliding down the scale, he nodded. "Then let's go."

They left the house and Glory locked the front door while Caleb dumped her stuff in his vehicle. He watched her head for her car and stifled the urge to persuade her to ride with him. He had bigger fish to fry in the argument department and he didn't think she was going to go down easily for what he had in mind.

Walking to her car, he leaned against the hood after she got in. The car light lit her profile. With her head in her hand as she propped her elbow against the steering wheel, she looked tired and lost, and he was filled with an absurd but overwhelming need to protect her.

"I think there's a hotel about a mile from here," she began, rubbing her forehead. "I can—"

"No."

She tilted her head to one side and raised her eyebrows. "No?"

The solution was crystal clear to Caleb, and he was confident Glory would ultimately agree. His jaw tightened ominously. Even if he had to throw her, kicking and screaming, over his shoulder to convince her. Meeting her gaze, he delivered his no-option plan in a calm but firm tone.

"You're staying with me."

Chapter Five

"Absolutely not," Glory said when she could find her voice. She should have seen this coming like a Mack truck, but her defenses were down and she was doing her best not to give in to a fit of tears. As soon as she checked in to her hotel room and Caleb left, she planned to have a good, old-fashioned, cleansing cry.

Since he'd arrived, he'd anticipated her needs with strength and a selective masculine sensitivity that drew her with appalling, insidious ease. She fought a thread of panic at the thought of being in such close proximity with Caleb. After all, she'd spent the past couple of days trying to put space between them.

She took a quick look at Caleb's expression. The dim interior car light didn't soften his face; he appeared about as flexible as granite. "It's very nice of you to offer," she said as politely as she could manage. "But this is your time off, and I don't want to intrude."

"It's not an intrusion. I have two extra bedrooms."

"I wouldn't want to interrupt your schedule. I'm sure you have some sort of plans."

"I don't have any plans," he said, shooting down that argument.

"Well, it's just not necessary," she said, groping for a valid excuse. "I don't—"

"This is about sex, isn't it?" Caleb cut in, his face lined with impatience.

Glory blinked. Trust Caleb to draw the bottom line.

"I'll make a promise." He leaned closer, and her heart tripped into double time at the intensity in his green eyes. "I won't push you into bed with me. When you're at my house, the only way I'll make love to you is if you come to me and tell me that's what you want." He tossed her a look of challenge. "Fair?"

Glory swallowed. There was nothing *fair* about the way Caleb made her feel, but even she had to admit his offer was as reasonable as they came. She nodded slowly. "Fair."

She saw the tension in his posture ease. "Let's go." He closed her car door and walked toward his vehicle, and Glory wondered how he'd managed to close the gap between them in less than twenty minutes without a single caress or kiss.

Glory awakened to the sound of a dripping faucet. It took a moment before she remembered she was in Caleb's town house. Her door was safely closed, but the bathroom light filtered underneath it, so she could make out some of the unfamiliar shapes in her room. The blue numbers on the alarm clock read 2:27.

She snuggled beneath the covers and yawned. Caleb's attempts to put her at ease had been awkward, but effective. He'd stuffed her with take-out Chinese food, and topped off her wineglass until she'd gone from relaxed to sleepy. A hot shower had finished her off, and she'd gone to bed early. He'd made a point of putting her in the room at the opposite end of the hall from his bedroom.

It was a curious fact that Caleb Masters had shown her more consideration in one evening than her husband had during their entire marriage. Curious and disturbing. Her body tensed at the thought of her ex-husband. Out of habit, she instinctively kept her body still, recalling his irritation at being woken in the middle of the night if Glory had suffered from a bout of insomnia. She had feared that he didn't like sleeping with her. At the end, her fear had been realized when he began to sleep in the guest room.

All that was over now. Sighing in exasperation, she flipped over and rearranged her pillow. She deliberately closed her eyes.

The faucet continued to drip. It might have been a soothing, monotonous sound if she hadn't been thirsty and if the darkness hadn't allowed her to think of Caleb. During the day, she could find a hundred ways to focus on something else. But in the darkness, her defenses lowered and her mind wandered where it wished.

He was an incredibly complex man. His kindness caught her off guard, and the sexual attraction between them made her cheek heat, even now, as it pressed against the cool cotton pillowcase. For just a moment she wondered if he would be happier with a woman in his life. A woman who appreciated his intelligence, but helped him remember the rest of what made him special. A woman who loved him and challenged him to remember his heart.

Her chest tightened at the thought. But she knew she wasn't that woman. She didn't have the strength or the fortitude to teach a genius about matters of the heart. And she didn't want to be that woman, she told herself. She absolutely didn't want to. Distress coursing through her like adrenaline, she listened to that drip and debated getting up for a drink of cold, cold water or counting sheep until she went back to sleep.

He was an idiot.

He never should have insisted that she stay at his house. Muttering an oath, Caleb covered his closed eyes. He could almost swear he could hear her breathe. *What an idiot.* For Pete's sake, the poor woman was down the hall with the door closed, probably locked. But he'd never been more aware of another person in his life.

Tonight he'd read her like a book. Although she'd tried to hide it, the sight of her damaged home had traumatized her. She'd been near tears until he'd urged food and wine down her. When she'd relaxed enough to yawn, he'd been oddly gratified.

Seeing her relax, however, had evoked another inexplicable response. He had wanted to take her up to his bed and hold her until she slept.

Caleb snorted at the notion. Even though he was an idiot, he knew he would want to do a hell of a lot more than hold Glory if she was in his bed. He wanted to taste her skin again and touch her breasts. He wanted to see her naked and wanting him. He wanted to thrust himself so deep inside her...

His body responded, and he swore again, throwing off the covers. He did *not* want to be aroused in the middle of a dark, endless night. If this was what it took for him to join the human race, he'd just as soon skip it.

As he sat up, he heard a meow of protest and a thump in the hall.

"Damn. Damn. Damn."

Glory clutched her throbbing knee and prayed she hadn't broken it. Rolling to her side, she swallowed a shriek of pain. She glanced around, but before she could find Fancy, the hall light flicked on and Caleb was walking toward her.

He wore a concerned expression, no shirt and skimpy gym shorts that eliminated many of her forbidden questions about his lean but powerful physique. Since he must be too busy to exercise regularly, she wondered why his shoulders looked so broad and muscular and how he kept his abdomen washboard flat.

He crouched in front of her and her heart skipped a beat. She didn't know which embarrassed her more, her immediate response to him or the fact that she was sprawled on his hall floor wearing a nightshirt. Mortified, she closed her eyes. "I hope I didn't kill your cat."

A meow sounded to her left, and Glory jerked her head to spot Fancy making her way over to Caleb to wrap circles around him.

He arched an eyebrow. "I think *she's* fine. What about you?"

"It's just my knee," she said, looking away from his bare chest and rising to her feet. She bit back a wince of pain. "I'm sure it'll be fine. I was going to get a drink of water and I must have startled her."

"Move it, cat, or I'm putting you on a diet." Caleb glared down at Fancy, then took Glory's arm and led her to the bathroom. "I think she's got a damn foot fetish."

Despite the pain in her knee, Glory laughed. "More likely her way of getting your attention. You don't have to—"

Caleb crouched in front of her again. "It's red. I better get some ice." He stood and filled a cup of water. "Here. Have a seat. I'll be back in a minute."

Holding the cup he'd placed in her hand, Glory sank onto the side of the tub. "I really don't—" she began, and broke off when she heard him on the stairs. All this fuss for a little drink of water, she thought miserably, and shook her head.

Bare moments passed before he appeared in the doorway with a bag of ice wrapped in a towel. She glanced up. "I'm sorry I woke you."

He shrugged and knelt beside her. "I wasn't asleep. It happens when I don't swim. This is gonna be cold," he warned her, then put the ice pack on her knee.

She twitched at the first shock and felt her spirits plunge. "You didn't get to swim because you were helping me with my disaster."

"I rarely sleep through the night. If I'm lucky a swim will wear me out, but not always." He cupped his hand under her calf and slowly stretched out her leg.

His intent concentration on her disconcerted her. Glory covered the commotion going on inside her by talking. "Sometimes I have trouble sleeping, too. My ex-husband used to get so angry when I woke him up by turning over."

Caleb frowned and met her gaze, his green eyes full of unasked questions.

"What?" Glory prompted.

"Why did you marry such a jerk?"

Taken aback, Glory hesitated, then gave a short laugh. "I guess I didn't know he was a jerk. He was involved with politics and it looked like he was really making a difference. I was so impressed with him. When he acted interested in me, I couldn't believe it." She thought back to when she first met Richard. It all looked so different now. "My mother was beside herself with joy that one of her daughters would marry a senator."

He narrowed his eyes. "You and your mom didn't get along. I remember your being upset about her once when you were tutoring me."

Surprised he would remember, she nodded slowly. "She wasn't very impressed when I was tapped for the National Honor Society. I think she wanted me to be more of a social success. We had different goals."

"You see her much now?"

"No," she said, and held her breath when Caleb skimmed his hand on the underside of her knee. It didn't mean anything, she assured herself.

"My mother and father moved to Florida. They didn't take my divorce well," she continued, and twisted her mouth wryly. "But my mother can console herself with the fact that my younger sister, Deidre, married a doctor, and they have a child." Glory felt a familiar pang. She didn't envy Deidre her doctor husband. A part of her, however, longed for a child.

Caleb twisted a lock of her hair and her gaze swiveled to meet his. *When had he moved closer?* She felt the heat from his body, his breath on her skin. But mostly she felt his comfort and compassion. His eyes searched hers.

"You've had a rough time, haven't you?" he asked in a low voice.

She took a deep breath and held it. "Yeah," she whispered, everything inside her waiting for... something.

He curved his hand around her jaw and shook his head. A wry half grin twisted his mouth. "In high school you wouldn't take anything from me. I liked you for that. That and the fact that you've never been a hardship to look at." His grin faded and his brow wrinkled. "You've forgotten how strong you are."

Glory was stunned. "You weren't supposed to notice,"she said breathlessly.

His eyes darkened, his gaze trailing over her body like a slow burn. "There isn't much about you I don't notice. Like the fact that you're wearing pink panties under that nightshirt."

His hand slid up her thigh and Glory's heart slammed into overdrive. "And your skin feels like silk." He leaned forward and nuzzled her hair. "And your hair smells like flowers."

Glory closed her eyes. His hands felt incredible, and his words were like chocolate to someone on a diet. She was starving for attention and approval, and he was fully willing to give it. It would be so easy to fall into his arms and bury herself in his body. So easy, yet so scary.

He slipped his fingers closer to her panties and pressed his lips against her cheek. How could a kiss on the cheek make her feel so needy? Would it be so terrible, she wondered, to give in to her needs just once?

Caleb sighed, and before she knew it, his warm hand had left her thigh and he'd pulled back. When she felt herself leaning toward him, she jerked back and opened her eyes. His face was taut with unrepentant arousal; he watched her and knew she was fighting the same arousal. She curled her fingers together to keep from reaching for him.

"How's your knee?" he finally asked in a rough voice.

Glory swallowed. "Numb."

Nodding, he stood.

Her emotions torn in a dozen different directions, she stood, too. "Caleb..."

He looked away from her and shook his head. "You need to get to bed."

She reached out tentatively for his shoulder, and he instantly stilled. She didn't know what to do or say, but the situation seemed unfair. This man had cared for her, and now he was going to bed the same way she was, hot and unbearably aroused. "I'm sorry I can't."

He lifted his hand. "Stop—"

"No," she said firmly. "I want to, but I just can't."
She softened her voice. "Thank you for accepting
that."

"This isn't acceptance, Glory," he said, not turning around. "It's waiting for the right moment." Then
he walked away.

After Caleb knocked her sideways with his parting
statement, Glory was certain she stood a better chance
of winning the Virginia Lottery than getting any sleep.
Fatigue won out, however, and she slept like the dead,
waking late in the morning.

She quickly showered and dressed, then washed
down a bowl of marshmallow-enhanced cereal with
juice. Making a mental note to call her insurance agent
and the realty office at lunchtime, she watched Caleb
amble into the kitchen wearing a blurry expression.
Sleep tousled and crabby looking, he pushed his fingers through his hair and grunted.

Glory struggled with a stab of guilt. Caleb might
often wrestle with insomnia, but she knew she was responsible for waking him last night. "Good morning," she said, and poured him a glass of orange juice.

"Thanks," he muttered when she offered it to him.
"How's the knee?"

"Blue," she told him with a grin, and turned to
rinse her bowl at the sink. "But my nylons are navy,
so no one but you, me and Fancy will know."

Leaning against the counter, he nodded without
cracking the slightest smile. "Are you always cheer-
ful in the morning?"

Despite his disapproving tone, Glory felt a measure
of sympathy for him. "I haven't ever really thought

about it. Right now I think I'm having a sugar surge from your cereal. Do you want some?"

"I can get it."

"No. It won't take but a minute." And it would give her something to do. He was like an irritated jungle animal, and she felt a strange urge to soothe him. As much as she'd like, after the way he'd cared for her last night there was no way on God's green earth he could ever be just a client to her.

Feeling his gaze on her every move, Glory took a deep breath and set the full bowl on the counter with a spoon. "Do you want to sit down at the table?"

Caleb shook his head and lifted the bowl to eat.

"You know," she said gently, "that's not the healthiest cereal on the market."

Caleb's mouth twisted. "It's the equivalent of sugar-coated cardboard, but it has marshmallows." He took another bite and swallowed. "And a man's entitled to at least one vice. The common choices are liquor, gambling and—" He flicked his gaze meaningfully over her. "Women."

Glory didn't want to know what color her cheeks were. *If you can't take the heat...* She cleared her throat. "In that case, marshmallows are fine." She glanced at her watch and walked toward the den. "I'd better get moving. What do you have planned today?"

Her idle question was met with complete and sustained silence. Glory turned back around and saw the blank, frustrated expression on his face. She winced, wishing she'd kept her mouth shut. "You don't know, do you? Caleb, you must have taken a day off every now and then."

He shook his head and set down the bowl. "Not in a long time. Then, I usually read professional journals."

Sighing, she tried to think of something. She hated seeing him at loose ends. "Okay. Why don't you play tourist today?"

"Tourist?" he repeated skeptically.

"Go to the Smithsonian. You can look at the antique cars or airplanes or dinosaur bones."

"Dinosaur bones," he said with not a flicker of enthusiasm.

His resistance was so thick she could cut it with a knife. She lifted her eyebrows. "If those don't interest you, then I'm sure you'd be fascinated by my favorite exhibit—The First Ladies' Inaugural Ball Gowns."

"Fascinated," he agreed in a dry voice, and walked toward her.

"Would you rather do something more constructive?" she politely asked, brushing aside her odd mix of feelings at his approach.

"I'm not sure," he said, tilting his head at a wary angle.

"Well, since you're joining the human race again, even if it's only a temporary visit, you might think about checking the three thousand messages you have on your answering machine."

They both glanced at the answering machine and the message light, which seemed to be blinking for infinity. Caleb scowled. "Where are those inaugural ball gowns?"

* * *

On the way to Caleb's house that afternoon, Glory decided to prepare dinner as a gesture of appreciation for his hospitality. After surveying his cupboard, she suspected his experience in culinary preparation was limited to cold cereal, microwave popcorn and frozen pizza.

She'd been uneasy about facing him this morning, but they seemed to have settled into a companionable relationship. Especially if she forgot about that comment he'd made about waiting for the right moment, and if she ignored how her pulse raced like buckshot when he was near. It would also help if she disregarded how attentive he was to her, and how much that appealed to her. Since she was professionally trained to sidestep problematic issues, it shouldn't be difficult to view Caleb as a friend.

If she reminded herself three thousand times a day, then she just might believe it.

Glory worked on forgetting, ignoring and disregarding that evening while Caleb watched her from across the kitchen counter as she prepared the food. She would have felt self-conscious if he hadn't been so eager to learn. The poor man was obviously bored out of his mind.

"What are you doing now?" he asked as she lifted the lid from the pan.

Glory stifled a groan. This was the tenth question he'd asked. She should have known a scientist would want an explanation for each step.

"I'm smelling Chicken cacciatore, and it smells ready." She served the meat on the plates.

He lifted his eyebrows. "You know it's done by how it smells."

"And by the clock," she said, adding the vegetables and pasta. "The recipe says to simmer for sixty minutes. You must have driven your mother crazy."

"Can't imagine what makes you say that." Without a cue from her, he walked around the counter and took the wine from the refrigerator. "I might have destroyed a few things before I learned to *manage my anger,* but..."

She took the bread from the oven and told herself she should resist. But she couldn't. "At what age did you learn to manage your anger?"

Caleb opened his mouth and hesitated. He studied her thoughtfully.

Glory chewed the inside of her cheek and aimed for wide-eyed innocence.

He cocked his head to one side and poured the wine. "You know, if you weren't my PR representative, unswerving in your efforts to expose only my most positive attributes, I might wonder if you were teasing me."

Tease. His voice made her think of sex. Her cheeks heated and she swerved around him to put the plates on the table. "I'm sorry," she said, backpedaling as fast as she could. "It's probably not nice to joke about—"

"Gotcha."

Glory glanced up and caught his arrogant expression.

He lifted his wineglass as if he were toasting her. "Might not be nice to razz your client, but it sure is fun, isn't it, Ms. Public Relations?'' He took a sip of wine. ''By the way, why's your face red?''

Glory sucked in an exasperated breath. For a moment she considered dumping the wine on his smartypants head, then reined in the scandalous urge. ''Caleb,'' she said with the shred of restraint she had left, ''you don't bring out the best in me.''

He shook his head, his expression changing in an instant. ''That's where you're wrong.'' His eyes serious, he skimmed his fingers just under the collar of her blouse. ''As far as I'm concerned, what's behind the politically correct talk and what's underneath that business suit is the best part of Glory.''

Glory closed her eyes at a gush of emotion. His hand felt good, his words even better. When had someone wanted her for her? She swallowed over her tight throat and opened her eyes to meet his gaze. ''When you say things like that,'' she whispered, ''you make it very difficult—'' The doorbell stopped her.

''I make what difficult?'' he asked in a rough voice.

She opened her mouth and the doorbell rang again. ''I—'' Her gaze slid to the door. ''Don't you need to get that?''

Caleb swore and pulled back. ''I want the rest of that statement. You hear?''

Glory blinked.

''Yes,'' he said emphatically, waiting for her confirmation.

''Yes,'' she managed to say, and watched him stride to the door. He jerked it open with no semblance of patience.

A tall blond man wearing a leather jacket, jeans and boots stomped through the doorway before Caleb said a word.

"You're here," he said in amazement to Caleb. "I went to the lab first, and they told me you'd be at home. But you're never at home. You practically sleep at that damn lab, so I didn't believe it."

"Ash," Caleb began, and Glory realized this was Caleb's younger brother. "What are you—"

Ash glanced down the hall past Caleb. His roving gaze abruptly halted at Glory. His jaw dropped, his eyes rounded. "A woman?" he said, his voice cracking in disbelief. "You've got a woman here!"

Chapter Six

Ash turned back to Caleb. "Well, hell, that explains why you're not answering the phone." He laughed. "What'd you do? Marry her?"

Caleb could have lived without his brother's sense of humor at the moment. Shooting a quick glance at Glory, he caught the turbulence in her blue-eyed gaze as she stared back at him. The moment was suddenly, shockingly, full of possibilities.

If he were different, if his life were different, she could have been his.

Years of denial kicked in. His emotions in a rampage, he shook his head to jerk his attention back to Ash.

"No," he managed to say at the same time Glory did.

He watched her vehemently shake her head, and squelched an odd sensation in his chest. "Glory's doing some PR work for me during my speaking tour. Her house got torn up in a storm we had, so she's staying here until she gets a roof over her head."

Ash rubbed a thumb over his mouth in a considering gesture and nodded. "Okay." He moved toward the kitchen. "Dinner smells great."

Ash's subtle way of wrangling an invitation. Caleb's mouth twisted as he recovered. His brother would beg, borrow or steal for a home-cooked meal. "Glory fixed it."

Ash gave her an assessing glance. "Why do you look familiar?"

"I went to the same high school you did. I was in Caleb's class."

Comprehension dawned. "That's right." He extended his hand. "You look even better than dinner."

Glory laughed; the sound was light, feminine and flattered. Caleb felt his shoulders tense. With his easy manner, Ash was the most socially adept of the Masters brothers. He had always been good with women. That fact had never bothered Caleb until now.

"There's plenty if you want to join us," she told Ash, and took another plate from the cabinet.

Before Caleb knew it, Ash was sitting at *his* table, eating the food Glory had prepared for *him* and pulling out all the stops to charm *his*— Caleb bit off an oath and wondered where in hell that thought had come from. Glory wasn't *his* anything.

None of his thoughts dispelled his dark mood. Despite Ash's propensity to show up unannounced, Caleb had always enjoyed his visits in the past. At the moment he was struggling with the urge to toss his younger brother's butt right out the door.

Ash flirted his way into second portions of everything. After he finished, he gave a sigh of satisfaction and glanced at Caleb. "Eli's getting married in a few weeks. He wants you to come. That's why I'm here. We couldn't get you on the phone."

Out of the corner of his eye Caleb saw Glory try to muffle a smile. "I was broadening my horizons," he said dryly. "Looking at the the First Ladies' inaugural ball gowns."

Ash looked bemused. "You don't say? And what's this about a speaking tour?"

"My director put me on temporary assignment."

Ash barked out a laugh. "I can't see it. I just can't see it."

"You and me both," Caleb muttered.

"He's done quite well," Glory interjected.

Ash shot her a look full of doubt.

"I guess you might say the first speech was a little rough," she conceded.

"It stank," Caleb told Ash.

Glancing upward for divine intervention, Glory rose from the table. "Well, the newspaper article was great. The reporter compared him to a modern-day knight."

Caleb shifted uncomfortably under the praise. "He'd had a few beers."

"Not that many," she said softly, and squeezed his shoulder as she took the plates to the sink.

Ignoring Ash's questioning gaze, Caleb stood. "You cooked. We'll do the dishes."

"It's no problem," she told him.

Caleb shook his head. "So let us do it. Thanks for dinner."

"You're welcome."

Her warm gaze met his, and he felt the kick of it deep in his gut. Struck with a compelling urge to take her in his arms, he shoved his hands into his pockets and nodded.

She cleared her throat and flipped her hair behind her ear. "I, uh, guess I'll make some phone calls."

"There's a phone in my room upstairs," he offered.

She nodded, then turned to Ash and smiled. "It was nice meeting you."

Ash stood and returned her smile full measure. "The pleasure was all mine."

Caleb clenched his fist at his brother's too-friendly tone. "G'night," Glory said, then left the room.

Sinking back onto his chair, Ash propped his feet on the chair opposite him and watched her leave.

Caleb chewed his ice as if it were glass. "You can stop making plans for Glory, right now."

Ash raised an eyebrow. "She's a great cook, and her body is—"

"Her divorce was final just six months ago." Caleb didn't want his brother talking about Glory's body. The mere hint of it made him feel inexplicably violent, and the strange emotion only served to irritate him more. "Leave her alone."

Ash studied him silently for a long moment. "Something going on between you two?"

Yes. No. Uncertain how to answer, Caleb hesitated, narrowing his eyes.

Ash was clearly busy drawing his own conclusions. "I thought you were all wrapped up in discovering the cure for Alzheimer's."

"Treatment," Caleb corrected, and felt a flicker of the ever-burning drive in his gut. He turned on the water faucet and shoved the dishes underneath. "I'm still committed to my research."

"But Glory's snagged your attention," Ash said, his face splitting into a wide grin.

Caleb scowled. "You don't have to look so damn happy about it."

"Oh, but I am. This is proof that you're a man, not a scientific machine." He shook his head. "Can't wait to tell Eli. I'll probably have to pick him up off the floor. Hell, he won't believe you're not living at the lab."

"I go back in a few weeks."

Caleb's grin faded. "So you're going back to twelve-hour days? You can't keep a woman like Glory when you're—" His face wrinkling in confusion, he dropped his feet to the floor and stood. "How do you plan to balance your lab schedule with whatever you're doing with Glory?"

Caleb rubbed his face. "I'm not doing anything with Glory. Yet," he added, because he knew something between them was inevitable. He hadn't thought about the future until now.

Leaning one elbow on the counter, Ash came at Caleb with an in-your-face bluntness. "So, what is this? Some kind of fling? She doesn't seem like that kind of woman."

"She's not," he said. That was part of the problem. Glory wasn't the kind for a quick roll in the sack, and he had a sinking feeling he wanted more than one night. It would take more than one time to know every inch of her inside and out. It would take more than one night for him to get enough of her, and that shook him.

The feeling was too private even to share with his brother. He flicked a quick glance at Ash. "I'll handle it."

Ash opened his mouth as if to argue.

"I'll handle it," Caleb repeated, and his quiet, hard tone silenced Ash. But Caleb still saw the questions in his brother's eyes, and he struggled with the disturbing notion that his sexual attraction to Glory was just the tip of the iceberg.

The following afternoon Glory burst through the door bracing herself for the upcoming evening. It was raining again, and her hair was drenched. Ready or not, however, she'd been ordered to represent the PR firm at a party tonight. She wished she had drafted the janitor to escort her. Then, at least, she wouldn't be facing her ex-husband's friends alone.

Cocktail dress in one hand, briefcase and bag in the other, she took a quick, calming breath when she saw Caleb and Ash in the den. "Hi. You two have a good day?"

Ash nodded. "I dragged Caleb to all the monuments." He chuckled. "It was like watching a kid take cough medicine."

"I loved every minute," Caleb deadpanned, then studied Glory while Fancy curled in his lap purring. "You ready for dinner?"

It was a crazy thought, but Glory wouldn't mind taking Fancy's place. The cat looked dry and comfortable. She was wet and frazzled. "Not tonight, thank you. My boss informed me that my presence is required at a charity function. And I think I'm going to have to perform miracles to get presentable." She gave a quick smile and tried not to think about the fact that she would probably see her ex-husband tonight. "I'll see you later."

After a quick shower she pulled on her robe and towel-dried her hair as she walked across the hall to her room. A spicy scent caught her attention and she lifted her head to find Caleb holding a drink and a plate with pizza.

"Here," he said, offering the plate.

Glory smiled despite her nerves. The considerate gesture touched her. "Thanks."

Caleb followed her into the guest room. His presence seemed appropriate at the same time that it unnerved her. "Tell me about this party," he said, and leaned back on the bed.

Feeling his gaze on her, she hung her towel over the hook on the back of the door and sighed. "It's for a good cause. I think it's to raise money for one of the homeless shelters downtown," she told him, and took a quick sip of the soft drink he'd brought her. "My company bought tickets, but everyone else was tied up tonight. So I was elected." She pulled a wide-tooth comb through her damp hair.

"You look like you're getting ready to go to the dentist."

Ever blunt. She almost laughed, but met his gaze instead. "Guess I'll have to work on that." She shook her head, wondering why she always felt safe yet oddly tense around Caleb. She felt she could tell him almost anything. "When I was married I went to so many of these functions, they began to blur together. I haven't seen a lot of these people in months, and that shouldn't matter, but..." *But it did,* she thought and took a bite of pizza to cover her discomfort.

"Your ex-husband might be there," Caleb said.

The pizza caught in her throat. Heavens, the man was perceptive. She coughed, then swallowed hard. "Probably," she admitted.

Caleb rose and handed her the drink. "You've never told me why you left him."

He was prodding, but his assumption that she hadn't been responsible softened her heart. "How do you know I was the one who left him?"

"Because he would have to be an idiot to leave you."

Her heart stuttered at the expression on his face. He wasn't touching her, he was standing five feet away from her, but he might as well have been kissing the breath out of her. A longing stirred and swelled within her. Closing her eyes, she hesitated. She'd kept most of the hurt to herself. "I left him when I found out I was a trophy wife, and he—" she opened her eyes and glanced away "—he wanted a different trophy."

She bit her lip, but the dam had broken and the rest of the story spilled out. "No matter what I did, I couldn't seem to please him. He liked the idea that I had graduated from American University and could speak French and Spanish, but he didn't really want me translating for him in public. He liked it that I was younger, but he always wanted me to dress older. I was very careful about what I said in public, to make sure I sounded supportive, but I always got the impression that he wished I had said something different.''

"Son of a bitch," Caleb muttered, his eyes full of fire. "Manipulating son of a bitch."

She opened her mouth to soften his assessment and realized even now that she was being careful. Though she fought it, some of the old feelings of inadequacy pulled at her. "I was almost relieved when he had the affair," she whispered, "because I don't think I could have stood living under the constant disapproval—"

He curled his hand around the back of her neck, stalling her words and breath. With a quick yet gentle tug he pulled her lips beneath his and kissed her. His mouth was warm, his tongue seeking.

His kiss blew her away physically and emotionally. It wasn't cool or calculated. Instead with each slant of his mouth, every stroke of his tongue, she felt his emotions slam into her. Passion and anger, tenderness and care. The combination was too seductive to deny.

Reeling, Glory splurged on the taste and substance of him. Her hands flexed at his broad swimmer's shoulders, his pounding heart vibrated against her chest and his heat, oh, she was sure she'd never be cold again.

Her knees dipped and he caught her, tearing his mouth from hers. Her lower body pressed firmly against his arousal, he held her with his gaze.

Silence, shocking and expectant, like the moment after glass shatters, rocked between them. His chest rose in rhythm with hers as they both caught their breath.

Glory was wordless. What do you say after you've been struck by lightning?

Caleb pressed his thumb over her swollen bottom lip and took another deep, shuddering breath. Then he closed his eyes, turned his head and set her away from him.

Glory concentrated on stiffening her knees, so she wouldn't fall on him. Hugging her arms around herself to keep from reaching for him, she held her breath and braced herself for whatever happened next.

Caleb shook his hair back from his face and narrowed his eyes as if he wasn't too sure about her anymore, as if he needed to keep his guard up. "Eat your pizza," he muttered, then left the room.

Glory stared after him. *Eat your pizza.* This? After the kiss of the century? After she'd wondered if he was going to rip off her robe and take her on the floor? Slumping, she shook her head and almost laughed. She would have if she hadn't still been trembling.

"Put your tongue back in your mouth," Caleb told Ash as Glory stepped into view. She looked good enough to eat. Her brown hair curved in silky, soft waves and she wore a white curve-skimming sheath dotted with pearls. At first glance, the dress was pretty in a tasteful way, but Caleb knew every man who looked at her would be wondering what she was wearing underneath it.

Ash tore his gaze from Glory long enough to give Caleb a double take. "Why are you wearing a suit?"

"I'm going with Glory," he said simply, and saw the quick flash of surprise in Glory's eyes.

As if he couldn't decide which way to look, Ash glanced at Glory, then Caleb, then back at Glory again. "You're going to let him out in public? He hates these things. He didn't even like parties when he was a kid. He—"

"At least I can dance," Caleb interjected in a mild tone.

Ash stopped, his mouth hanging open for another second before he clamped it shut.

Caleb twisted his mouth at his brother's response. For all Ash's social skills, he had two left feet on the dance floor. Feeling Glory's gaze, he looked at her.

Her eyes were curious, cautious and, unless he imagined it, relieved. "I guess I am letting him out in public," she said with a slow smile, then lifted her eyebrows. "You know you're going to be bored out of your mind," she warned him.

"I'm prepared for all eventualities." It was convenient that she was agreeable, because he would have insisted. Although he couldn't explain it to himself, let alone to anyone else, after she'd told him about her ex-husband, Caleb couldn't *not* go.

"Okay, let's go."

She turned toward the front door, and Caleb heard a muffled moan from Ash. He caught sight of the back of her dress and struggled with his own primitive response. A deep V revealed a tantalizing glimpse of the honey-colored bare skin of her back.

"G'night, Ash," Caleb said meaningfully, and opened the door for Glory.

Ash just nodded.

When they stepped outside, he turned to Glory. "This isn't dressing older, is it?" he asked, referring to the comment she'd made earlier about her ex-husband.

"No." She grinned with a flash of her lost defiance.

Caleb felt the kick of it all the way down and knew he was in trouble.

The first hour at the hotel ballroom was uneventful. Caleb shook hands and tried to be friendly with a dozen curious Washington socialites and their husbands.

"Here comes Maris the witch," he warned in a low voice when he recognized the woman approaching them.

Glory shook her head chidingly. "She's not really—"

Caleb lifted an eyebrow in skepticism. "It's her middle name. Where should I lick you this time?"

Glory gave an appalled laugh and color stained her cheeks. "Don't even think about it. Don't even—" She cleared her throat. "Maris, it's nice to see you. You're looking lovely tonight." She gestured toward Caleb. "I'm sure you remember Dr. Masters."

Maris gave a little sniff. "Indeed. One of my charity groups is planning a fashion show next spring. I've been asked to find a local firm to handle the publicity, and I thought of you."

Glory looked stunned. "Well, thank you. I need to discuss it with my manager, but I'm sure he'll be interested."

Maris nodded. "I'll give you a call next week." She slid her glance back to Caleb. "It's good to see you again, Dr. Masters."

"Indeed," Caleb returned, and felt Glory's elbow in his ribs. "Glory's told me many good things about you."

Maris brightened. "I've always said Glory's a sweet young woman," she said, and added a few more pleasantries before she left.

Wearing a surprised expression, Glory turned to Caleb. "You handled that very well."

"You expected me to call her a—"

She held up a hand to stop him. "Let's just say you have been known to be a little blunt."

"A little." Caleb's lips twitched at the understatement. "This time I wasn't. Does this mean I get to lick you now?"

"No! Absolutely not." Amusement and exasperation warred in her facial expression. "Go get something to eat while I try to drum up some business."

Caleb didn't see anyone in the vicinity that looked threatening, so he agreed. But he kept his eye on her from his seat at the bar. When one of her firm's clients engaged her in a drawn-out discussion, his mind began to wander, so he snatched a paper napkin and scratched out a chemical equation he'd been playing with lately.

Before he knew it, thirty minutes had passed. He quickly glanced around and found Glory talking to a tall, distinguished man. On second glance, he saw that she wasn't talking, she was listening. She wasn't smiling, either. Caleb narrowed his eyes at Glory's tightly clasped hands and ramrod-straight posture.

A dark suspicion burned in his gut as he strode toward her. He caught the end of the man's soliloquy.

"And with the campaign coming up, I'm hoping you won't allow yourself to be drawn into making negative comments. You know how the press can be."

"Glory is a master at avoiding negative comments. I give her practice every day," Caleb interjected, then smiled and wrapped his hand around Glory's waist from behind. "I lost track of you," he told her.

She glanced up and Caleb saw the relief in her eyes.

The man cleared his throat. "Your escort?" he asked, his voice shaded with disapproval.

Glory glanced back at him and Caleb felt her take a careful breath. "Dr. Caleb Masters," she said formally, "this is Senator Richard Danson."

Danson extended his hand and Caleb watched the politician take his measure. "Medical doctor?"

Caleb shook his hand. "Research, Grayson Pharmaceuticals," he said, and did his own quick and dirty evaluation. Tall, distinguished, a little gray at the temples, impeccably groomed, the man was smooth and probably anal retentive.

Obviously familiar with the company name, Danson lifted his eyebrows and nodded. "Excellent company." He gestured toward Glory. "I'm sure Glory has mentioned me."

"Not much. To tell you the truth, I've always equated politicians with used car salesmen, so I don't keep track of the guys who change office every two years."

Glory made a little choking noise.

Danson stiffened. "Six years," he corrected. "I'm in the Senate."

Caleb shrugged, enjoying the man's flush. "Whatever."

"Caleb is researching a new treatment for Alzheimer's disease," Glory managed to say in what Caleb suspected was a valiant attempt to change the subject.

Danson nodded and made an appropriate murmur of approval as a good senator should, then turned back to her. "I didn't know you were seeing anyone."

Caleb roared with laughter.

Glory and Danson gaped at him.

"By the time the ink was dry, the line was forming," he said wryly. Bonehead. Caleb swallowed the insult for Glory's sake. He was counting her respirations to make sure she didn't faint. "I'm sure you know a woman like Glory doesn't come along in a man's life more than once."

Ready to terminate the conversation, he held Glory against him snugly. "I think that's our song," he said to her, then nodded at Danson. "Later."

He practically carried her to the small dance floor. When she met his gaze, she looked shell-shocked. *"Our song?"*

Caleb placed her limp hand on his shoulder and tugged her closer. "It's as good as any. What is it?"

She blinked, but sluggishly followed his lead. Her forehead creased in concentration. "I think it's 'I Left My Heart In San Francisco.'"

"I've never been. Have you?"

"Once," she murmured. "It rained."

"You're pale," he said. "You're not gonna faint or anything, are you?"

"No," she said, looking him in the eye again and shaking her head. *"The line was forming?* Have you lost your mind?"

Caleb grinned. "I was inspired," he told her dryly.

She closed her eyes and her feet finally caught the rhythm of the music. "I still can't believe you called him a used car salesman."

Caleb looked at her with concern. "I technically didn't call him a used car salesman. I compared him to one."

She opened her eyes and regarded him skeptically. "Delayed diplomacy?"

Caleb's lips twisted. "Not much chance of that. Glory, why in hell did you marry such an idiot?" he asked bluntly, because his supply of socially acceptable conversation was depleted.

She threw back her head and dissolved into laughter. The sound was soft and light. Utterly feminine, he thought as he savored the sensation of her in his arms. Utterly addicting.

She could be mine, he thought, and the urge to possess, to give and take, burned beneath his skin. The thought was difficult to deny, impossible to dismiss. When the dance ended, he was still burning.

Within minutes Glory suggested they leave. They thanked the sponsors for the party, then Caleb drove home. When he pulled in to the deserted parking lot, he killed the engine and sat for a moment, drumming his fingers on the steering wheel. His body was coiled with tension. His mind was busy compartmentalizing.

He'd spent the evening pretending Glory was his woman. Pretending they were physically and emotionally familiar. *Intimate.* Glory's acquaintances and ex had bought it. Unfortunately, his body had bought it, too.

Caleb had never been good at pretending.

"I'm gonna sit out here for a minute. You can go in if you want." He offered her his keys.

Glory glanced at his hand, then, wearing a curious expression, she cocked her head to the side and looked at him. "That's, okay," she said, and cracked her window. "The temperature's dropped a little and I could use a moment to unwind, too."

Taking a deep breath, she shifted in her seat, tilted her head back and sighed.

Caleb watched her. No way in hell was he going to unwind with her sitting less than fourteen inches from him. Her lipstick was gone, and her hair drifted over one eye in appealing disarray. She looked touchable.

He clenched his hands.

"So, how crazy did that party make you, anyway?" she asked in a soft voice.

"I don't attend parties very often, especially society functions, so it was fairly easy to tell myself it would only last a couple more hours."

She reached for his hand, and Caleb's gut tightened. It was just a casual touch, he told himself. She didn't know how she affected him.

"Well, you surpassed all my expectations tonight. You were terribly, terribly—" Smiling, she leaned forward and kissed him lightly at the corner of his mouth. "Wonderful. Thanks."

It took less than a millisecond for Caleb to realize that she was flirting. A new confidence glimmered in her eyes, her smile teased, and looking at her made him feel predatory.

Glory was feeling her oats, and Caleb wanted to feel them, too.

Before she backed away, he turned his head, putting his mouth inches from hers. Her quick intake of breath was like an intimate caress. Unable to resist just one taste, he kissed her, drawing on the soft texture of her lips. He flicked his tongue over her bottom lip, then pulled back.

Her eyelids were at a sexy half-mast. Her gentle sigh blew over him. It cost him, but he warned her off.

"You need to go in," he told her in a gruff voice. However, he couldn't bring himself to remove her hands from his shoulders.

"Why?" she asked, not showing the sense to back away even an inch.

He sucked in a quick breath and drew in her perfume. "Because I want you," he said bluntly. When she still didn't pull back, he swore and shook his head. "I'm not smooth. I'm not what you're used to."

Her gaze locked with his for a timeless instant.

"Thank God for that," she whispered, then slipped her hands to the back of his neck and pulled his head down. When her mouth met his, he was stunned. When her tongue slipped past his lips, he felt as if he'd been torched.

Chapter Seven

She'd drunk only one glass of wine, but Glory had a delicious buzz, and Caleb was responsible. For the past two years of her life she'd felt old and unattractive. But after the way Caleb had held her and looked at her tonight, she felt feminine, powerful, alluring. And she liked it.

She liked it so much she didn't want it to stop.

Sliding her tongue against his, she decided she liked the way Caleb tasted—dark, potent and a little reckless. He pulled her against him and she liked the way his muscles strained beneath her fingertips. His chest was hard against her breasts.

He deepened the kiss and his hands skimmed the sides of her breasts, sending a quiver of titillation through her. She arched against him, wanting to feel more of his heat and male need.

Caleb groaned and dropped his mouth to her throat. "You don't know what you've started," he muttered.

Then the world turned upside down and he tugged her across the console at the same time he jerked his seat back. He was nearly reclining, and Glory sprawled in his lap, her hands braced on his chest. She swayed slightly away from him, and the steering wheel at her back nudged her toward him.

The position was novel to her and it gave her a moment's pause. Mesmerized, she stared into Caleb's dark eyes. His fingers curled possessively around her hips while his hardness nudged between her legs, sending the blatant message of his need. Holding her, he rocked against her intimately.

Her breath seemed to stop. She should be shocked, should be pulling away. Instead, Glory felt a knot of pleasure and tension form, low and deep inside her. The tips of her breasts grew tight. Her skin was hot and her heart beat an uneven tattoo. She closed her eyes at the overwhelming sensations.

"Did you know that I wanted you this much?" Caleb asked in a low voice as he moved his hips again.

Glory sucked in a sharp breath and shook her head.

"Does it bother you?"

Her eyes shot open. "No, I just..." she managed to say, then got lost in the intensity of his gaze. He pulled her upper body closer to his and she swallowed. "My heart was beating so loudly I wondered if you could hear it," she whispered, because whispering was the best she could do.

A ghost of a grin tugged at his lips. Holding her gaze, he shook his head and slowly pushed her dress down past her shoulders, down so that her breasts were bare to him. His eyes growing still darker with arousal, he looked his fill then pressed his ear against her chest. "I hear it now," he murmured.

The gesture was so tenderly erotic it hurt.

He rubbed his cheek over her breast then took her nipple into his mouth.

Glory bit her lip at the sharp sting of desire that coursed through her. "Oh, my—"

Caleb pulled back with obvious effort. "Too much?"

Yes. No. Not enough. "Please don't stop," she said, overwhelmed.

Caleb's face went taut with raw passion, and he took her mouth with his at the same time that he pushed her dress up her legs. His mouth was avid and hungry, his tongue thrusting with the age-old rhythm of sex.

Dizzy with longing, Glory tugged at his loosened tie and shirt buttons, craving the texture of his bare skin. Caleb circled her thighs with purposeful hands.

He pulled away and swore softly. "God, I hate the man who invented panty hose. I'll buy you more," he promised, then pushed his finger through her stockings.

Glory felt the shredding sensation of sheer nylon, then his fingers moved with shocking deliberation past her panties to her moist femininity.

"You're hot and wet," he muttered in rough approval as he slipped a finger inside her. "And tight."

Her body clenched, but he didn't give her time to breathe. He lowered his mouth to her breast and laced his tongue around the beaded tip.

Her mouth went dry as dust. She couldn't remember ever being wanted this much. She couldn't remember wanting this much. It distressed and thrilled her. With each stroke of his hand and tongue the world seemed to spin and everything inside her tightened.

Clinging mindlessly to Caleb, she heard him swear when headlights from another car flashed across them. Folding her close to him, he swore again. "Hold on," he told her.

Her short breaths chased air into her lungs. She tried to clear her head, but her body was still thrumming with urgency and she could still feel Caleb's hardness between her thighs. Her swollen breasts were nestled into his chest, and she was trembling.

Glory was struck with an appalling urge to cry. "I must be out of my mind," she whispered to herself.

Caleb relaxed his grip. "Why?" he asked against her ear.

She blinked at the burning sensation in her eyes and the tightness in her throat. "I completely lost track of where we are. For heaven's sake, we're in a car, and we practically—"

Caleb laughed, but the sound was rough around the edges. "No, we didn't. I'm still completely dressed, and I'm still hard as hell."

She searched his gaze, but she couldn't read him. Was he angry? Had she offended him? Was he blaming her? *He had warned her. He had tried to stop her.* She bit her lip. "I—I'm sorry. I should have stopped sooner. I should have—"

Her words dried up when he set her away from him. She instantly felt the loss.

He slid her dress back into place, then pulled back and plowed his fingers through his hair. "You let go, and now you're regretting it."

She frowned at the accusation in his tone. "I didn't say I regretted anything," she told him, although her head was so muddled she wasn't sure what she felt.

His green eyes narrowed in perception. "Then what would you say? I'm sure you've got a politically correct comment for this situation."

Glory stared at him as if he'd slapped her. He'd held her in the palm of his hand. He'd made her feel wonderful. Was he really that upset because she'd come to her senses, or was something deeper going on here?

Something deeper with Caleb? She lifted her hand to cover her eyes, wishing she could make sense of this. When she realized she didn't have a prayer, she followed her only possible course of action and pushed open the door.

Caleb's hand stopped her. "Ash will still be awake," he told her, and she wished his voice wasn't so gentle. "You might want to fix your hair before you go in. You look—"

"Like I almost had sex in a car," she said, shocking him into silence with her own bluntness. She pulled down the mirrored visor, jerked her fingers through her hair and rubbed the mascara from beneath her eyes. Her lips were swollen, her cheeks pink. She looked *wanton*.

Frustrated, she slapped the visor back into place, feeling the weight of his gaze. "Forgive me for not knowing the proper social etiquette after I've been kissed senseless. It's been a while. Like forever," she muttered, and got out of the car. Furious that her knees were shaking, she swore under her breath.

"Glory—"

"Jerk." She slammed the car door and rushed to the town house. Murmuring good-night to a bewildered Ash after he opened the door, she dashed up the stairs, washed her face and brushed her teeth and was in her room within five minutes.

Her heart pounding, her chest tight with disappointment, she stripped off her dress and tossed her ruined stockings into the trash can. Turning off the light to avoid her reflection in the bureau mirror, she tugged on her nightshirt and stared at the bed. *Fat chance of getting any sleep tonight.* And tomorrow, she recalled with a sense of dread, she and Caleb were scheduled to fly to hot, humid New Orleans.

Her mind twisting like a tilt-a-whirl, she sighed and climbed into bed anyway. It was the sensible thing to do, and, unlike earlier tonight, Glory usually chose the safe, sensible path.

Caleb was not a safe, sensible choice. He was temperamental, blunt to the point of pain, at times distracted, and too passionate for his own good.

Too passionate for her good, a tiny voice inside her chided.

Footsteps in the hallway interrupted her thoughts. Certain it was Caleb, Glory lay still, hearing him stop outside her door. She held her breath. Moments passed, then he continued down the hall.

Glory let out her breath, but she couldn't have said if she was relieved or disappointed.

* * *

The next morning Caleb dodged Ash's questions and promised to be in North Carolina for Eli's wedding in three weeks. He noticed Glory made herself scarce until it was time to leave for the airport.

The flight was torture. Excruciatingly polite, she avoided his gaze. He wanted to talk to her, but a friendly grandmother took the third seat in their row. He was so damn distracted he couldn't focus on the professional journal he'd brought with him.

He'd misunderstood her. It was crazy, but getting that close to her and bringing her that close to the top had made him feel too much. Caleb was unaccustomed to dealing with any sort of tender feelings. Passion for his research he understood. Passion for Glory drove him crazy. Her response had shaken him and he'd been so aroused he couldn't see straight.

He scratched the word *jerk* in the margin of his journal, then slid a glance over to Glory. She was talking to Grandma as if her life depended on it.

Rubbing his chin, he pulled out a sheet of paper and wrote a few more words. This time, however, he wasn't writing chemical equations.

Later that night, after Caleb delivered a mediocre after-dinner speech and answered questions, impatience and frustration nagged at him. He put off an interview and escaped to his room.

Stripping off his shirt and tie, he planned to go to the hotel pool and swim laps until his legs cramped. A knock on his door stopped him halfway through his belt buckle. "Who is it?" he demanded.

A long pause followed. "Glory."

Caleb pinched the bridge of his nose. The woman was going to wreck him. He strode to the door and jerked it open. "What?"

Dressed in a conservative navy suit that could have been stamped I Mean Business, she still managed to look wholly feminine. He noticed her navy stockings and thought about the ones he'd shredded last night. He noticed every visible inch of her, but it was everything that made her a woman, physical and emotional, that alternately fascinated and drove him to the edge.

She lifted a piece of paper. "Got your note from the bellman a few minutes ago."

Wary, he shoved his fists into his pockets. "Yeah?"

She gave him a long-suffering glance. "Are you going to invite me in?"

"I was going for a swim," he told her, but she walked past him into the room anyway.

Sighing, Caleb pushed the door closed and leaned against it.

"You said, 'You're right. I was a jerk. But I'm not used to being kissed senseless by a beautiful woman.'" Her voice softened. "'And I'm not used to holding pure gold in my hands.'" She looked up from his note and her gaze searched his. "Did you mean it?"

"You ought to know by now that I mean what I say."

Her eyebrows wrinkling in confusion, she stepped closer to him. "Then why are you acting this way?"

Caleb rubbed his face. "I suppose you want me to use 'I' statements. I'm tired," he told her. "I feel cranky." *I want you.* He bit his tongue. The sooner she was out of here, the better.

"Did you eat dinner?" Concern laced her tone. She must have seen him hesitate, because she turned and headed for the phone. "I'll call room service and—"

Caleb reached for her. "I need to swim. I have too much energy and I need to get rid of it."

Glory slowly turned back around and slid her fingers through his. She took a deep breath. "Maybe I can help."

Staring at her small hand intertwined with his, Caleb stood perfectly still. There was only one way Glory could help tonight. After last night, though, he needed it spelled out. "How?"

Color rose in her cheeks, but she met his gaze. "Maybe I can help you get rid of your energy," she said huskily.

"How?" he asked again, and this time his voice was rough around the edges like his nerves.

Glory tentatively skimmed her hand up his chest. "I guess I could start by kissing you senseless," she suggested with a smile that wrapped around his heart and squeezed.

Certain he was hallucinating, he touched her hair to make sure she was real. "And then what?"

She stretched her arms around his neck and pressed her soft body against him, and Caleb was suddenly, intimately aware that she was real.

"We keep going until we pass senseless," she finally said, and kissed him. Her fingers stroked his bare chest like butterfly kisses in a caress designed to soothe.

Caleb, however, was hungry. His blood raced with the need for immediate gratification, instant ease, but he made himself stand still for her tender assault.

His physical response was primitive, but he understood it. Biology, he comprehended. His unstinting drive to possess her unsettled him, but he could accept it.

It was the way his heart tripped when she sighed in pleasure, however, that confounded him. His craving for her smile made no sense. His overwhelming desire to make her see herself the way he did perplexed him.

The unerring knowledge that one time with her wouldn't be enough disturbed him.

With Glory so intent on pleasing him, though, Caleb couldn't remain disturbed or perplexed. His skin heated as her fingers shimmied down his ribs to his abdomen. Instinct overrode his good intentions and he deepened the kisses until she moaned and pulled away for air.

Her eyes were glazed. "Senseless yet?" she murmured, and took his mouth again before he could answer.

Her tongue moved in an erotic invitation he couldn't resist. Tugging loose her buttons, he pushed off her jacket, then unsnapped her bra and dropped the clothing on the floor. The sensation of her unfettered breasts against his chest forced a groan from his throat.

Go slow. Go slow. Go slow. He mentally chanted the words like a mantra while his body grew rigid and his breath shortened.

When she pulled sweetly but ineffectually at his belt buckle, something inside him ripped wide open. Sucking in a shallow breath, he ditched the rest of her clothes, then pulled her up into his arms and carried her to the bed.

For a moment all he could do was look.

Naked, her brown hair spread out on the bedcover, her blue eyes brimming with passion, she reminded him of a conqueror's prize. Her breasts were small, rose tipped and creamy, her body slim yet womanly. Surely there were more beautiful women in the world, he thought. Why couldn't he imagine one?

Lifting up on one elbow, she motioned him closer with a smile. "I'm not certain how it happened, but I had on more clothes than you when I walked into this room, and now I have none."

When Caleb stepped in front of her, she pushed aside his hands and took a millenium to unbuckle his belt. He began to sweat. "Let me finish," he offered.

Glory shook her head and put her hands inside his slacks to push them down.

"You're going to kill me," he told her, closing his eyes.

"Too slow?" When he nodded, she started on his briefs. "Maybe I need a little practice," she said, and seconds later he was as naked as she.

Her lips feathered against his hipbone and he found it excruciating to watch her head so close to his throbbing hardness. Just a breath away.

She slid her hands up his thighs, then to the front where she cradled him in her palm.

A wounded groan of longing came from deep inside him.

She moved her thumb over his shaft and he jerked.

She lifted her gaze to his, and her desire to bring him pleasure was written in her eyes. "What do you want?"

"Everything," he told her. "I want to know every inch, every secret." He shook his head. "But I can't wait. I want inside," he said, lifting her hands to his mouth, then following her down to the bed. "Inside you." He settled himself between her thighs and took her mouth.

She pulled back breathlessly. "We need something from my purse," she managed to say. When he didn't move, she said, "Condom."

The necessity sank in and he rolled to her side. He grabbed the slim navy purse and handed it to her.

She pulled out the square packet, tore it open, then looked up at him. "Can I put it on you?"

His heart stopped. *Could she know? Could she possibly know she was a dream come true?* He swallowed and lay back on the bed. "Yeah."

She stretched the thin sheath over him, her touch making his sensitive flesh throb. Reaching for her, he brought her mouth back to his and fondled her hot, moist femininity with his fingers. She was like a budding flower beneath his touch, set to burst into bloom any minute.

Savoring her naked body, he stroked her inside and out until she began to tremble. "Caleb," she entreated him raggedly.

"You're not ready," he protested, wanting more, wanting everything.

He stroked her again and felt her ripple of pleasure. She bit her lip. "Yes, I am," she insisted, moving her thighs apart in invitation.

She was vulnerable, exposed, and the sight of her glistening femininity affected him like a live wire.

Locking his gaze with hers, he positioned himself between her thighs and thrust inside her as deep as he could go. Encircling him like a tight, wet glove, Glory arched toward him. It was his turn to tremble. He watched her until he felt her convulse around him, and her shudders sent him straight up to the sky.

Ten minutes later he'd caught his breath enough to speak. "You're incredible," he said, pulling her against him. "You're beautiful."

He felt her secret smile against his throat. "Are you sure you're not in a sex-induced stupor?"

"No, that was earlier," he confessed. "I wanted to tell you how beautiful you were, but my mouth wouldn't work."

"Could have fooled me," she said, and slipped her hands up his arms. "I thought your mouth worked fine."

Her bangs fell over one of her eyes and her sexy, playful gaze met his. Caleb felt an odd tightening in his chest. "I've never told another woman she was beautiful," he said, because although the teasing was fun, he wanted her to know.

Her grin slowly fell and she lifted her hand to his cheek. "Thank you," she said, a dozen emotions deepening her blue eyes. He wished he could read them all.

The next morning Caleb woke to the sight of the bright sun streaming through the curtains. Glory nestled against his side, still sleeping.

He lifted his head to look at her. Her hair was tousled, her lips swollen, and the white sheet was tucked beneath one of her pretty little breasts, baring it to his sight.

He liked the way she looked.

One of her legs was entwined with his. He could feel her slim belly against his side, and one of her hands rested on his chest. Her breaths were soft and regular. He rubbed his hand lightly over her bare hip and felt a ripple of pleasure when she undulated closer.

He liked the way she felt.

The day marked a first for him. Although he'd been to bed with a few women, he'd never woken up with one. He'd never wanted to.

For a forbidden moment he wondered what it would be like to wake up in the morning, every morning, with Glory in his bed. The image taunted, seduced and unsettled him. He pushed it aside.

Glory's eyes fluttered open. She gave a sleepy sigh and rolled slightly away. Drawn to her warmth, Caleb followed.

"Mornin', Glory," he murmured, brushing a strand of hair from her face.

She smiled, slowly and softly. "Mornin', Caleb. Did you miss your swim last night?"

Caleb chuckled and, because he wasn't inclined to resist, he kissed her. Her uninhibited response sent a rush of arousal through his blood. Pulling her on top of him, he took a deeper drink of her, skimming his hands over her back and bottom.

The first time they'd made love had taken enough of the edge off that he could explore her the way he wanted. The second time he'd gotten high from the sound of her crying his name. The third time, just a couple of hours ago, had been leisurely and easy, until he'd lost it at the end.

He shook his head at his erection. "I want you again," he told her.

Her eyes softly glazed, she shifted her hips, and the tip of his hardness pressed against her moist entrance.

Caleb groaned and rubbed himself against her. "Oh, Glory, what am I gonna do with you?"

"I don't know," she murmured, clearly enjoying the friction of his movements. "You feel—" She stiffened and her eyes widened. "I just remembered I don't have any more protection."

It cost him, but Caleb stilled. Caught somewhere between torment and ecstasy, he tried to be practical. "Is it a bad time?"

She frowned in concentration. "I think it's too late, but—"

"I'm clean," he assured her.

She closed her eyes and Caleb knew she was feeling everything he did. Feeling the thunder of his heartbeat, the promise of sweet intimacy.

"Studies suggest that it takes twenty-four hours to replenish an adequate supply of sperm necessary for conception."

She opened her eyes and laughed in frustration. "That is the worst excuse for not using contraception I've ever heard."

Maybe. Probably, he thought, but he couldn't pull away from her. "Your call," he told her.

Glory groaned. "I think it's too late," she said, as much to herself as to him. "I don't think I can get—" Gazing at him, she shifted slightly and he slipped just inside her. "Oh, my. I've never been on top," she confessed in a whisper.

"Is that a yes?" he growled, his nerve endings screaming.

She sank the rest of the way onto him. "Yesss."

They were inseparable for the rest of the weekend. For breakfast she talked him into café au lait and beignets in the French Quarter. That evening after his speech, he dared her to eat a crawfish. When the sun went down, they drifted into a nightclub and listened to an hour of smoky, sultry jazz.

For a man who wore tension like a second skin, Caleb seemed relatively relaxed. For a woman who doubted herself, Glory felt more self-confident and complete than ever. They meshed together so well it was almost unearthly.

If he'd given her half a moment to think about the strength and depth of her feelings, she might have gotten scared. But Caleb took every waking and non-waking moment.

Glory pushed back the vague sense of unease she felt during their final approach to National Airport. The spell between them remained unbroken until their plane landed and Caleb began to load her suitcase into his cab.

Glory laughed. "Wait a minute. I'm going to *my* house."

Caleb turned to her and frowned. "What about your roof?"

"The real-estate agent got off to a slow start, but they said it should be fixed over the weekend. Livable by Monday. That's today."

He shoved his hands into his pockets and looked away from her. He looked edgy, unsettled, yet deep in concentration. His head jerked toward her and he pinned her with his gaze. "Why don't you just move in with me?"

Glory's heart jumped into her throat. She stared at him, lifting her fingers to her mouth in shock. "This is—" Her voice failed her and she shook her head. "I don't know what to—"

"Do it," he told her, the expression in his green eyes rocking her world. "Move in with me."

Chapter Eight

"No."

Sheer self-preservation forced the word from her throat. Glory swallowed hard. "I can't—"

The cabbie honked his horn, but Caleb stepped closer to her. "It makes sense," he said, his tension, his determination rolling off him like a wave. "I want to be with you, and I've only got a few more weeks before I go back in the lab."

And what happens after you go back to the lab? A hard knot of distress crowded her chest. "Everything happened so fast. We haven't discussed any future plans," she managed to say, and heard the cabbie shout at them. "I can't think straight."

Caleb looked as if he didn't understand.

Glory sighed in frustration. "I can't make the decision to move in with you while I'm standing on the curb at National Airport. I just can't. And that cabbie's going to drive off with your luggage if you don't respond to him."

Swearing under his breath, Caleb told the driver to let the meter run, then turned back to Glory. His turmoil was so thick she thought she could have touched it. Wordlessly he picked up her luggage and motioned to the cab behind his.

Again Glory was filled with the urge to soothe and reassure. She could deal with her own upset, she just hated to see his. "It was a wonderful weekend," she told him. "You made it wonderful. I—"

Caleb turned and pulled her against him. Lowering his mouth, he gave her an eye-popping, possessive kiss that lasted a full minute. When he drew away, Glory had to blink to regain her equilibrium.

"We'll talk later," he said tersely, then got into his cab.

Glory managed to climb into her own cab, but as the driver headed toward her home, she wondered when her head would stop spinning. She walked through her front door as if she were walking on someone else's feet.

Determined to dispel the cloud of confusion inside her, she concentrated on the repairs made to her house. The upstairs carpet had been replaced. The bedroom and hallway smelled of fresh paint. The roof was patched, the windows replaced. A new set of mattresses took the place of the old ones.

Telling herself everything would return to normal now, she walked through the rest of her house, but it seemed foreign to her. She looked at the bare spot on her den wall and made a mental note to get her picture from Caleb, because deep down she knew she wouldn't be moving in with him.

Sinking to the sofa in her quiet den, she leaned back and closed her eyes. She had underestimated what making love with him would do to her. She had expected pleasure, but she had never imagined she'd be swimming in a flood of emotions she didn't understand.

Glory had always known she wasn't cut out for casual sexual relationships, so her experience was limited to her marriage. In the clear light of day she couldn't exactly say why she'd made love with Caleb. Maybe it was his unapologetic need. Maybe it was her own desire for approval.

She had never been wanted like that before. She had never wanted like that before. Images swirled in her mind. Caleb's grin. His eyes darkened in passion to forest green. His hands and mouth, tender and demanding.

Her heart caught and a moan escaped her throat. If only it was just sex. But it wasn't. It wasn't the words. It wasn't the technique.

It was the man. The way he made her feel. The way she thought she made him feel.

God help her, he'd made her fall a little bit in love with him.

"What a mess," she whispered, apprehension twisting through her. If she was in love with him, she was crazy. For all his attentiveness to her, Glory knew Caleb was a man with a mission. A modern-day conqueror. Caleb might laugh, but Glory agreed with the reporter who'd compared him to a knight. It was as if he'd made an oath to find a treatment for Alzheimer's, and he would dedicate his life to carrying out that oath.

Move in with me, he'd said.

For a while.

Though she'd been stunned, she must have heard the rest of the sentence even though he hadn't said it. *Move in with me.*

Until I go back to the lab.

He wasn't promising something he couldn't deliver. There was a definite end note to this song, she knew. A sweeping sense of loss made her heart heavy. She couldn't love him just for a while or until he went back to the lab. She wasn't strong enough.

The moment he walked through her front door that night for dinner, Caleb knew Glory wasn't his anymore. For one brief rational moment he wondered when it had happened. Somewhere in the airspace over D.C.?

For the first half of the meal he wrestled against his conclusion. Everything between them had been so right. They had clicked together like complementary chemical compounds. His impatience suddenly kicked in with a vengeance. He set down his fork and pushed away his plate. "Why don't you just go ahead and dump me?"

Glory stared at him wide-eyed. Her fork clattered to her plate.

Not that she'd eaten much, he thought, idly noticing her nearly full plate. Waiting silently, he watched her take a quick swallow of wine.

She shook her head. "Why would you say that?"

She was taking the long way around, Caleb concluded, and steeled himself for the discussion from hell. "You haven't touched me. You've avoided looking at me. And our conversation has centered around the weather, your roof and Fancy."

Feeling a rough anger pulse through him, he narrowed his eyes. "I may be a social blockhead, but this weekend I was closer to you than I've ever been to another human being, and I would have sworn you liked it."

Glory flinched.

Caleb swore under his breath. "Are you going to tell me you regret it?"

"No!" she immediately said, her gaze finally meeting and holding his. Caleb saw a well of emotion in her blue eyes and felt a scrap of relief.

"I don't regret the time we had together." She looked away again and stood. "Not really," she said, and his gut twisted. "I guess there are always consequences, and now we have to deal . . ." Edging closer to the dining room window, she took a breath. "With those consequences."

Lord, she confused him. He stood, too. "Such as?"

She bit her lip and made a searching gesture with her hand. "Well, feelings," she said quietly, and glanced at him. "And plans."

He fought a surge of frustration. She was using that very controlled voice that annoyed the hell out of him, but her gestures said she was nervous. He chose the rational approach. "That's why I asked you to move in with me."

"It isn't that easy."

"Why not?"

"Because you're going back into the lab in a few weeks." He could tell she was making a deliberate effort to remain calm.

"So?"

Her chin lifted and her eyes flashed. "So how are you going to have a relationship with a woman when you're working eighty hours a week?"

Everything inside Caleb came to a screeching halt. He stared at her for a long moment, the seconds ticking between them. "I don't know."

He saw a slice of pain come and go in her eyes before she looked away. "I think I do know," she told him. "You once told me you wouldn't ask for anything long-term, because you just couldn't."

"Other men who work in the lab have relationships with women. Some even have wives." Shoving his hands into his pockets, he cursed the lack of conviction in his voice.

"You aren't other men, though, are you?" she asked and he heard a tremble in her voice that wounded him.

"We've got weeks before I go back."

"I can't," she said, and bit her lip. "I just can't. I'm not put together that way. I'm not set up for a temporary affair."

He cocked his head to one side, trying to understand her. "Let me make sure I understand this. You're saying unless we get married, you won't see me anymore."

"I didn't say that. I'm not ready for marriage," she wailed, looking as if she was nearing the end of her rope. "Maybe I'm not ready for anything."

Caleb frowned, feeling an ominous tightening in his gut. "How do you explain this weekend?"

Her eyes dark and desperate, she shook her head. "I can't explain it. I wanted you and you wanted me, and it happened."

"You're not making sense," he told her bluntly. It was the only civilized comment he could form at the moment. Everything else that came to mind involved throwing her over his shoulder and hauling her back to his house.

"I'm sorry."

And Caleb knew he'd been right. She wasn't his anymore.

He drove to the health club and swam lap after lap after lap, punishing his body as he tried to clear his mind.

He tried to strip the vivid images from his memory, but his too-clever-for-his-own-good brain wouldn't permit it. He'd held her, made love with her, laughed with her. She'd been his.

He should be relieved, he thought as he walked into his quiet town house late that night. The prospect of an ongoing relationship with a woman had always seemed incredibly burdensome to him. He absently petted Fancy when she circled his ankles.

The hollowness in his gut was hunger, he told himself. He didn't want to belong to anyone, and he sure as hell didn't want anyone belonging to him. The hollow sensation persisted, however, after he ate the microwave pizza he'd prepared.

He went up to his room to change his clothes, pausing as he passed the extra room where Glory had stayed. Irritated with himself, he pushed open the door to prove it wouldn't affect him.

But a remnant of her scent hit him and his body reacted as if she were right there with him. The objective scientist in him found the response curious. He noted the way his heart rate picked up and his skin warmed. His nostrils flared as he drew in another breath of air with the teasing residue of her perfume. His muscles grew tense. His entire body tightened in anticipation.

The very human male swore.

Caleb had never questioned the choices he'd made for his life before, and he was angry that he felt forced to do so now. Forced to examine what had always been a given. Forced to question what had always been absolute.

His choices were still correct, he decided, hardening his resolve. It was his purpose in life to solve chemical problems that could change human lives. He'd been born for it, would have taken an oath for it.

Sucking in a sharp breath of air, he gritted his teeth and ruthlessly squelched his response. Just as he turned to leave, his gaze snagged on the picture Glory had brought from her house the night of the storm. He hadn't taken a close look at it until now.

In the tradition of folk art, the artist had painted a mother and young child overlooking the Shenandoah Valley. The scenery was beautiful, but what caught Caleb was the way the mother held the child in the circle of her arms and gently smiled as if the two shared a secret.

The hollow sensation gnawed at him again. He'd never wanted or needed human connections. They got in the way. He'd never been curious about human relationships. His interest had been held with unrelenting ease by his research. He stared at the picture and thought of Glory, and Caleb wanted to know the secret.

Glory was late, and the little white stick had turned blue.

Three mornings in a row.

She'd denied the possibility for a few days, but her monthly cycle was as regular as a calendar.

I'm pregnant.

Thirty years old, college educated, unmarried and *pregnant*. When she wasn't horrified, she was totally embarrassed. She should have known better, should have shown more sense, should have used her brain.

All the *should haves* in the world weren't going to do her one bit of good when she tried to explain this to her supervisor. Single motherhood wasn't politically correct in Washington, D.C.

Wanting to crawl into a cave and hide for the rest of her life, she sat staring at the screen of her laptop computer in the middle of the night in a hotel room in Pittsburgh. Since she couldn't sleep, she was trying one last time to revise Caleb's speech. It had become a ritual for her to rewrite his speech, then watch him read part of it and discard the rest. He'd never read her speech word for word.

I'm pregnant.

She felt her stomach roll.

Her nausea was related to stress, she was certain. It was too early in the pregnancy, and nausea was most likely to hit whenever she thought about trying to tell Caleb. Still, she kept a package of saltines close by.

"Oh, Lord," she muttered, squeezing the bridge of her nose. When she thought about Caleb, her heart hurt. When they were apart, it was crazy, but she missed him. When they were together, she missed the way it had been between them. Their conversations were brief and painfully polite. During the flight this afternoon they hadn't spoken more than two or three sentences to each other.

I'm pregnant.

How was she going to tell him? A part of her wondered if she should. His life was clearly mapped out, and this was not part of his plan.

Glory shook her head. She wasn't going to settle this at 2:00 a.m. Tearing her thoughts from Caleb, she focused on the speech. She needed to focus on the speech, on the very reason she was going to have to take this pregnancy, trimester by trimester, alone. Though her throat was tight, her fingers skipped over the keys, forming words and sentences until she finished. She hit Print, and while the mini bubble-jet printer did its job, she flicked off the light and crawled beneath the covers.

Glory knocked on Caleb's door again and glanced at her watch. The lack of sleep had gotten to her, and she'd given in to a quick nap after lunch. Now they were running late.

He whipped the door open. "Yeah."

Seeing the glazed expression in his eyes, she would have bet a month's salary he'd been working. He was seeing her, but not. He wore jeans, a T-shirt and no shoes. The sight of his bare feet tugged at her. "You're not dressed," she told him.

He blinked. "The speech."

"You're on in thirty minutes."

"Give me five," he said, and shut the door in her face.

Glory looked at the ceiling and sighed in frustration. She supposed she should be thankful he didn't invite her into his room. The proximity would have wreaked havoc on her already jumpy nerves. But Glory was struck with the sad knowledge that Caleb was rapidly returning to his old ways.

She checked her pocketbook for crackers and drummed her fingers against the wall for a couple of minutes before his door whipped open again. Striding out of the room with his speech rolled in his fist, he tugged at his unknotted tie and swore.

Glory hesitated, then stepped forward. "Let me." She concentrated on making the Windsor knot with the crimson silk, but the tension he emanated nearly overwhelmed her. His chest was hard beneath her fingers. She could practically feel his blood pump through his veins, and, as always, she was drawn to his heat.

Where had her breath gone? She bit her lip and glanced up at him. "There."

His gaze was taut, intense as it traveled over her face. "You smell good."

Feeling a crazy kick inside her, she smiled and backed away. "Thanks. We'd better go. Did you get a chance to read over the speech?"

They walked toward the elevator. "No. I've been doing a little bit of work."

"Cheating?"

He jerked his head toward her and frowned. "Cheating?"

She searched his green eyes. "Weren't you supposed to wait until next week? Isn't that when you're scheduled to go back?"

Caleb looked away, and she felt as if a door shut between them. "I've had some time on my hands," he said as the elevator arrived.

Minutes later Glory sat in uneasy anticipation among the members of Pittsburgh's Junior League Women's Club. Caleb was a wild card this afternoon. He'd been so distracted on the way over she'd wondered what he would say once he opened his mouth. Of course, some would say that was part of his charm. Taking a deep breath, she watched as he stepped up to the microphone.

"Good afternoon," Caleb said with a nod. "Thank you for your interest and support in our search for a pharmaceutical treatment for Alzheimer's disease."

She wished he would smile.

"Approximately two million people are diagnosed with Alzheimer's disease. I could tell you numbers and statistics, and we could discuss genetic research." His mouth twisted in a brief grin. "I'll leave the genetics to my brother, Dr. Eli Masters. He's always been more patient."

A wave of gentle amusement fluttered across the room, and Glory raised her eyebrows in surprise. It was a miracle. He was reading the speech word for word.

"My pressing interest is in the lowered levels of essential chemicals that the brain needs to store, process and record information. Up to now, chemical treatments have . . .''.

Glory listened, relaxing slightly. Feeling a tinge of melancholy, she fastened her gaze on him and took in every movement, every gesture. This was almost their last speech together. It would all be over soon. Even when she told him about the pregnancy, Glory knew it wouldn't change the course of Caleb's future. That was set.

Still amazed that he was following the script, she reached for one of her saltine crackers and watched Caleb continue to read. ''. . . nerve growth factors and the regeneration of damaged brain cells. I'm pregnant. This could change the—'' He broke off and frowned, staring at the paper.

Stunned silence filled the room.

Glory's heart pounded in her ears. She crushed the cracker in her hand and stared at Caleb in disbelief. *He hadn't really said that.* She'd just imagined it. The stress was getting to her and she was hearing things.

But Caleb's gaze latched on to hers with the force of a heat-seeking missile. ''I'm pregnant,'' he repeated.

The room began to spin. Glory felt her blood plunge to her feet. Her chest was so tight she couldn't breathe. For a terrible moment she feared she would faint. She desperately wished she could slide down between the cushions of her chair and disappear. But even in her agitated state, she knew that wasn't likely.

In the corner of her mind she registered the high-pitched giggles and muffled snickers. Rising to her feet, she slipped toward the side door and did what women in distress have been doing for centuries.

She went to the ladies' room.

Chapter Nine

Glory was pregnant. The knowledge jerked the rug out from beneath him. His heart twisting in a square knot, Caleb watched Glory steal out the side and restrained the urge to follow.

For all of a minute.

Taking a deep breath, he forced himself to turn back to the tittering group of women. "It is, of course, physiologically impossible for me to be pregnant. I wanted to see if you were paying attention." He forced a grin, then skipped over the next two pages of the speech. Quickly reading the last page, he nodded and left while the audience was still applauding.

Swiftly winding his way through the hall, he searched in vain for Glory. Frustration grated at him. He felt as if he were a machine and someone had thrown a stick in his moving parts. Everything inside him was off-kilter.

He noticed several women coming out of the rest room and stopped one of them. "I'm looking for a thirty-year-old woman about so tall." He held his hand to his chin. "She's got brown hair down to her shoulders, and blue eyes. She's wearing a black-and-white—"

"Checked suit?" she asked. When he nodded, she pointed toward the rest room. "She looked a little pale."

Caleb bowed to social convention approximately thirty seconds, then pushed open the door to the ladies' room. Striding past two gaping middle-aged women, he spotted Glory immediately. Out of the corner of his eye he absently noted a woman who was applying lipstick extend the color down her chin while she did a double take.

At that point Glory glanced up, a damp paper towel pressed to her forehead. If anything, her face turned whiter. "Oh, my God," she whispered. "What are you doing in here?"

"You're pregnant," Caleb said, wondering, but not really caring, how the rest room had cleared out so quickly. "You look like hell."

"Thank you."

"Are you going to faint?"

She closed her eyes and sank onto an upholstered bench. "I wasn't before you came in."

Torn between clutching her to him and howling, he struggled to keep his voice level. "Why haven't you told me?" He wondered if she'd planned to keep it from him. The notion made him crazy.

"I just found out," she said, biting her lip. "Kind of. I haven't really adjusted—"

Caleb's brain clicked into overdrive. "What do you mean, kind of? Have you been to the doctor?"

Glory shrugged and looked away. "No. I haven't been to the doctor yet. I took one of those at-home pregnancy tests. Well, actually, I took three. It was positive every—"

"And you didn't tell me after the first one?"

She blinked. "I wanted to wait until I adjusted to the idea." She looked at him in exasperation and stood. "I hadn't figured out *how* to tell you. What was I supposed to say? Oops. You're not only a genius, you've got super sperm. Happy Father's Day."

Caleb put a clamp on his impatience. *You're going to be a father.* He couldn't fathom it. His body was nearly crackling with adrenaline, but he struggled to approach her in a rational manner. "What are you planning to do now that you know you're pregnant?"

"Do?" She looked at him in confusion, as if she didn't comprehend his question, as if there'd been no choice, never any doubt. When the light dawned, however, her eyes glinted with anger and she tossed the paper towel into a trash can. "I'm going to have the baby," she said, her voice rock hard with determination. "Don't worry, I won't ask anything of you."

Something inside him eased now that he realized she wasn't considering an abortion. At the same time, however, her other statement popped his cork. "Why not?" he demanded. "I'm the father. You should be asking anything of me. You should be asking everything of me. Dammit, for that matter, we should get married.''

Glory stared at him, and he could tell she was almost as shocked by the suggestion as he was.

''Do you realize you just proposed to me in the ladies' room?''

Caleb would have bitten a nail in two if there'd been one available. ''It was expedient,'' he growled.

She shook her head and laughed without humor. ''Oh, well, that's a terrific reason to spend the rest of your life with someone. Because it's expedient. The answer is no.'' She picked up her purse from the bench and took a quick glance in the mirror.

Caleb's chest felt as if it was in a vise. ''I care for you,'' he said, wishing for once that he had some experience articulating his feelings. ''I care for you more than I've cared for another human being.''

Her gaze met and locked with his in the mirror. Her blue eyes searched his for something. He wondered if she found it.

She pressed her lips together and sighed. ''You don't love me,'' she said quietly.

He wouldn't have thought it possible, but his chest twisted tighter, as if he'd swum for hours. ''I care for you,'' he said, because he wasn't sure what love was. When her gaze fell from his, he touched her shoulder. ''You shouldn't have to raise this baby alone. I don't believe you want to.''

''Oh, Caleb, who's to say that if we got married I wouldn't be parenting this child by myself, anyway. Think about your hours. You've said it before. Because of your research, you *can't* make a long-term commitment. I'm not even sure you're wired to have a family.''

Her argument cut him, but he couldn't dispute it. He wasn't sure he was a great candidate for a husband. In fact, he'd always steered away from the possibility. He didn't have a clue how he would adjust, but down deep in his gut he knew he would have to. He smoothed his hand through her hair. ''Things are different now,'' he said in a low voice.

''You mean, it's expedient because I'm pregnant.''

Her shoulders were stiff with tension, but she didn't resist when he tugged her around. ''I missed you. I can't go in the guest room anymore,'' he confessed. ''It still smells like you, and thinking about you messes up my head for hours.''

She glanced at him tentatively, as if she were measuring the risk. *Should* she gamble on him? he wondered. He saw a glimpse of hope and emotion so deep it rocked him, before she closed her eyes.

''Oh, I don't know, Caleb. I just don't know.''

He pulled her into his arms and ached at the sweet sensation of her closeness. ''You don't have to decide this minute.''

She relaxed.

''I'll give you five.''

Glory made a sound between a sob and laughter and shook her head. ''I don't know what to say.''

Say yes, he wanted to tell her, but the uncertainty in her eyes stopped him. He stifled a curse. ''Say you'll think about it. Say you'll try to work this out with me.'' Too full of feelings he'd never experienced before, he narrowed his gaze at her in wonder. ''I want to help take care of you.''

Her eyes widened and turned shiny with unshed tears. She blinked quickly. "Okay," she said in a husky voice. "I'll think about it."

Caleb felt a fraction of his tension ebb, and held her against him. He wanted her close. Even a foot away was too far. He rubbed his mouth against her hair and reacquainted himself with her scent. His mind was racing a mile a minute. He wondered if she was frightened. He wondered what a pregnant woman needed. He wondered what a wife needed.

The sound of a toilet flushing broke the silence.

Glory and Caleb glanced up as a woman appeared from one of the stalls.

She washed her hands and shot Caleb a long, considering glance. Then she grabbed a paper towel and looked at Glory. "I think you should marry him."

"This isn't necessary," Glory told Caleb for what seemed like the zillionth time. He had insisted on riding home in the taxi with her from the airport.

He didn't bother to argue; instead he put his arm around her shoulders and ran his fingers through her hair. The gesture tugged at her heart.

"You okay?"

"Fine," she assured him. "Fine." His attentiveness chipped away at her defenses, but Glory was determined not to follow one misstep with another. She'd just picked herself off the floor from one bad marriage. "I could have gone home by myself."

"Uh-huh," he said without a lick of conviction.

She glanced at him skeptically. "Is this your way of humoring me?"

He stretched his long legs. "I'm showing restraint, but I'm going to look after you. Get used to it."

Blunt again, with no apologies. Despite his gentleness, there was a steely resolve in his tone. Glory shivered, uncertain how to deal with it. Twenty-four hours ago she would have sworn she would be taking on the adventure of parenthood all alone. However unromantic his proposal had been, Caleb had knocked her sideways with the mention of matrimony.

She never would have believed it. Even now, though she knew it was motivated purely by the fact that she was pregnant, she wondered if he felt more for her than she had expected. She wondered about possibilities. She wondered why it was so easy to lean against him and hope. Whatever the future, Glory couldn't find it in herself to completely cut him out. She couldn't change the fact that he was the father of the child she carried. The knowledge made her stomach dip every time she thought of it. She didn't know which way her relationship with Caleb would go, but she knew they would be bound for years by their child.

When the cab pulled in to her driveway, Caleb carried her suitcase into the hallway, then all the way up to her bedroom. He set the luggage down on her bed, then turned back to her. Shoving one of his hands into his pocket, he gazed at her in silence, and Glory was struck anew by how much she was drawn to him.

"Thanks," she said to break the silence.

He nodded, moving toward her. "Sure you won't change your mind about coming home with me?"

Glory shook her head, but her stomach fluttered when he curled his hand around the nape of her neck as they walked back downstairs.

"You look a little tired. You gonna get some sleep?"

"Yes," she said, feeling a pinch of amusement.

"And you're gonna make an appointment with your doctor?"

"Yes." They came to a stop at her front door.

"And you're gonna marry me," he stated more than asked.

Glory opened her mouth, then closed it. "I'm going to try very hard to consider everything and make the best possible decision."

Frustration tightened his jaw. "Okay," he said, and took her off guard by pulling her into his arms and kissing her.

His hands were firm but gentle as they cupped her chin and urged her to respond. His fingers massaged her jaw, coaxing her to open for his tongue, and Glory's heart hammered against her rib cage. It was a tender, thorough kiss that whispered of deeper emotions, yet screamed, *Baby, you're mine*. It was a reminder of sweet intimacies.

By the time he pulled back, Glory was trembling. She swallowed. "Why'd you do that?"

His green eyes glinted with sensual determination. "You said you planned to consider everything. I wanted to make sure you didn't forget *everything* you need to make your decision."

With no answer for that, Glory blinked and opened the door. This was going to be more difficult than she'd dreamed. "When do you go back to the lab?"

"Wednesday. I'll be in touch," he promised, and strode toward the waiting cab.

Glory nodded, but part of her was filled with doubt. *We'll see,* she thought, instinctively bringing her hand to her womb. *We'll see.*

He called or saw her every night that week. Friday night he showed up at her door with a pizza. "I have better health insurance," he told her as he strode past her to the kitchen.

Glory bit back a smile. Every conversation had begun with Caleb pointing out another reason they should get married. "How do you know that?"

"I told my benefits coordinator I needed a comparison between my group health and your company's group health for maternity."

"I thought we agreed we weren't going to tell anyone yet."

His face was the picture of innocence as he opened the box. "I didn't."

"Don't you think they're going to consider it a little strange for you to be asking about maternity benefits?" She shook her head. "I wonder how many times it's gone around the grapevine by now."

Caleb frowned. "No one has said a word to me. As a matter of fact, my director told me to keep doing whatever I've been doing that's put me in a decent mood." He tossed her a sexually meaningful glance. "I've got my orders."

Not willing to touch that one with a ten-foot pole, she poured soft drinks and grabbed some plates. "Bet your insurance has some sort of preexisting condition clause," she told him, joining him at the table.

"Not for pregnancy. You are keeping track of all the information I'm giving you, aren't you?"

"You mean the federal tax break for joint-filed tax returns, the advantage of one mortgage versus two and the advantage of a two-parent family when one of the parents gets sick?"

Caleb nodded. "And don't forget the great sex."

Glory swallowed a bite of pizza whole and glared at him. "I'm trying to be rational about this. I would think you'd appreciate that."

"I do," he said. "I'm just helping."

Glory wasn't sure she would survive his *help*. Although he insisted he wanted to stay and watch a video with her, halfway through it she caught him scratching notes on a piece of paper. She might have thought he was completely absorbed if it hadn't been for the slow caress of his fingers on the back of her neck.

He sat close to her with his thigh against hers and her hip tucked to his. In the darkness of the room she was constantly aware of him, his scent, his breathing pattern, his touch, his heat, and it all had the same effect on her as some kind of subversive, wicked foreplay.

As soon as the movie ended he leaned back and pulled her to him. She felt the pressure of his hardness against her thigh and caught her breath. "I could have sworn you'd forgotten I was here."

His eyes intent, he brought her mouth to his. "You underestimate your effect on me," he muttered against her lips.

The way he held her made it easy to respond. The way he touched her made it easy to forget about being rational and careful and prudent. The way he kissed her made it easy to forget about everything but him.

His hands slid over her with the confidence of a man who'd paid attention. He knew where to touch her and how to make her burn. Her heart was racing and the feminine knot of longing she'd denied for the past weeks grew tighter with each stroke of his hands, each thrust of his tongue. He slipped his hands beneath her shirt and bra to her swollen breasts. When his fingers flicked over her nipples, the electric sensation made her cry out.

Her unrestrained reaction made him hesitate. He pulled back and looked at her with dark, questioning eyes.

"They're really sensitive. My breasts," she added. "I—I guess it's the pregnancy." She was having trouble thinking, so she looked away from him. "Other women have mentioned—" She swallowed. "Other pregnant women say their breasts get extremely sensitive."

"Because of the pregnancy," Caleb said, his voice rough with fascination, and he gently stroked her breasts. "Does it hurt?"

Biting her lip, she met his gaze. The sensation was excruciating. "Not really hurt. It's just almost too much."

"Too much?" He gently fondled her nipples, and a moan broke from her throat. She arched against him. "God, you're sweet," he muttered, sensual surprise lacing his tone. "If I put my mouth on you, I bet you'd climax," he whispered.

"Caleb—" She meant to protest, but he'd already moved and his warm, moist mouth rendered her speechless. She had never been so shockingly, easily aroused. Every time he touched her it was as if an invisible thread was attached from her breasts to her nether regions, and the coil of tension inside her became nearly unbearable.

He suckled the distended peak, his tongue laving her with tender, merciless strokes. The coil inside her suddenly snapped, and Glory jerked, feeling the suspended rush and Caleb's arms tighten around her.

A long moment passed before she could breathe, let alone think. She had been utterly shameless, completely out of control. Embarrassment swept over her and she tried to duck her head against his chest.

"Hey," he said, sifting his fingers through her hair. "What's going on here? What are you doing?"

Glory couldn't look at him. "I just didn't expect..." She shook her head. "This is so embarrassing," she whispered.

"What—" He broke off and swore. "C'mon, look at me. What are you talking about?"

Glory reluctantly lifted her head. "I just lost it."

His lips twitched. "Yeah. You ought to do it more often." When she rolled her eyes, he shook his head. "No. I mean it. That was one of the most erotic experiences I've ever had. Watching you was almost enough to make me—"

He searched her face and must have read her uncertainty. A hint of wry masculine frustration flickered across his eyes. He sat up and pushed a hand through his hair. "Almost is the operative term."

Glory struggled with a ridiculous surge of guilt, and tried to explain. "I just don't know how much, how far," she amended, "we should go until we decide what we want to do."

Caleb raised a dark eyebrow. "There's just one problem with that," he told her. "I already know what I want." His gaze made it plain that what he wanted was her. Glory pressed her lips together at her ambivalent feelings. She still had too many doubts, too many questions, too many fears.

Caleb rubbed a hand over his face and stood. "I don't know how we're going to fix this. You're scared spitless to marry me, and I'm trying like hell to reassure you."

"I'm sorry."

He held up his hand. "My brother Eli's getting married next weekend. I want you to come down to North Carolina with me."

Glory stared at him in surprise. "Why?"

He shoved his hands into his pockets and turned to face her. "I know this has been a shock for you, and you're scared. And I know it's your body that's gonna be changing. But this is a first for me, too, Glory." He thumped his chest. "I've never suggested marriage to a woman. I've never helped make a baby. I don't know where I stand with you," he said, his temper beginning to show. "But you're pretty damn important to me, and I want what's left of my family to meet you."

"I'll go," she said immediately, because her heart simply wouldn't let her say no.

"What did your doctor say?" Caleb asked as they drove past the North Carolina state line.

"Dr. Hill said I'm normal and pregnant. She examined me and took blood. Then she prescribed prenatal vitamins, gave me a bunch of material to read on pregnancy and told me the due date would be in March.''

Caleb slid his glance over to her and took her hand. ''March is a good month to be born. You mind letting me see the literature?''

''Okay.'' Her stomach fluttering, Glory smiled in response. Sometimes she still didn't believe there was a tiny human growing inside her. She had so few physical signs, although she'd noticed that she'd felt a little more tired than usual the past couple of days. ''Dr. Hill said I might be able to hear the heartbeat next time.''

Surprise flickered across his face. ''That's incredible. This early?''

''Around ten or twelve weeks.'' She hesitated. ''Do you want to come?''

''Yeah,'' he said, as if the thought hadn't occurred to him. Then his face grew serious. ''It's been a while since I brought this up.''

''At least two days,'' she murmured, already knowing what he wanted to discuss. If her heart hadn't felt ripped in two different directions, she might have found his persistence amusing. But Glory still wasn't sure about marrying Caleb, and wanted so badly to be sure. She wondered what ''benefit'' he was going to bring up this time. Last time he'd passed along the fact that six diaper services delivered to his home, while only two delivered to hers.

''I've thought of something else you should consider. If you don't want to go back to your job after the baby is born, you could free-lance from home.''

It wasn't *I love you, I can't live without you,* but it was more significant to her than diaper service.

"That's a good point," she said, and changed the subject. "Tell me about your brothers."

A short while later they pulled in to Eli's driveway and Glory got her first glimpse of the house, a dark two-story monstrosity that frankly looked, well, creepy. She and Caleb walked up the cracked concrete entrance and rang the doorbell, which sounded like a gong.

A little boy holding a child's boom box pulled open the door, and a barking dachshund skidded to a stop beside him. The boy looked solemnly from Glory to Caleb, then cracked a grin that stretched from ear to ear. "It's Uncle Caleb," he yelled. "And he brought a lady!"

Within seconds Caleb's brother Eli appeared with his arm wrapped around the waist of his fiancé, an attractive woman with a ready smile. About the same height as Caleb, Eli was runner lean with lighter, shorter brown hair. They both had the trademark Masters green eyes, but where Caleb emanated a magnetic tension, Eli reflected a more restrained energy.

There was nothing restrained, however, about the the obvious love in his eyes when he looked at his fiancé, Andie Reynolds. Even at first glance, seeing the two of them together made Glory's heart twist.

They hugged Caleb, then welcomed her in a friendly, curious manner. "We're glad you could come," Andie said as she led them into the house. "The house probably scared the bejeebers out of you when you first saw it, but don't worry, it's not haunted, it's just a decorator's nightmare. I'm working on it."

Eli glanced past them to the car. "Amazing," he said, seeming surprised. "You turned off the ignition and the lights."

Confused, Glory shot Caleb a questioning glance. He sighed and muttered, "Later."

"Ash will be here in a little while. We got your measurements, so your tux is ready," Andie told Caleb. "Rehearsal's at the church at six-thirty, followed by the rehearsal dinner. Then I think Ash might have something planned for you guys while my friend Samantha is taking me out."

"Heaven help us all," Eli said.

Andie gave him a light punch, and he pulled her into his arms. "You just remind Sam that us Viking explorer types don't take kindly to having our women led astray."

"Viking explorer types?" Caleb echoed, keeping his hand at Glory's nape. She wondered if he realized how possessive the gesture was.

Andie just shook her head in response to his question. "You'll have to meet Sam to believe her. We'd love you to come with us," she said to Glory. "It won't get too crazy. I need my beauty rest for tomorrow," she said with a grin.

"Did you bring me a carburetor?" Eli's son, Fletch, demanded.

Caleb bent down to his nephew's level. "I brought you a computer motherboard this time."

"Oh, wow!" Fletch's eyes grew wide as saucers. "Where is it?"

"In the back seat."

Eli snagged Fletch before he could tear out the door. "What do you say?"

"Thanks." Fletch gave Caleb an enthusiastic hug, then ran down the hall.

"I wondered why you didn't bring him a truck or a fire engine," Glory mused, staring after the little boy. She would never have dreamed of getting a five-year-old such a gift, and realized Caleb had shown a great deal of thought.

Andie and Eli exchanged a knowing glance. "It's a real challenge to keep up with Fletch's curiosity level. He's very bright," Andie explained. "Listen, let me show you to your room. One good thing about this house is there are a ton of rooms."

Feeling Caleb's gaze on her, Glory glanced up as he bent closer. "Okay?" he murmured near her ear.

Physically, yes. Emotionally, she was in a tailspin. "Fine," she assured him, and followed Andie upstairs. The moment when Caleb had hugged Fletcher froze in her mind. It was suddenly easy to imagine him hugging their child just like that. The image was clear and right. It didn't answer all her questions, but it showed the possibilities. Possibilities too far-reaching for her to consider right now, she knew, and tried to focus on her hostess. "I hope it wasn't a problem for Caleb to bring me. I'm sure you're incredibly busy with the wedding."

Andie shook her head. "It's no problem. My family decided to rent a couple of suites at a hotel so they could have a little privacy." She led Glory into a room at the end of the hall. "Caleb will be right across the hall," she said, hesitating for a moment as she studied Glory.

"I don't want you to feel pressured," she began in a warm, gentle voice, "but we're all very pleased that

Caleb brought you. Especially Eli. He's hoping this is a sign that Caleb has found some kind of balance in his life. Last year when Caleb visited, he just really wasn't here.''

Swallowing her amusement, Glory walked toward the window and nodded in understanding. ''I know what you're talking about, but I'm not sure Caleb's attitude toward his research and 'balance' go together.''

Andie made a wry face. ''Eli gets like that every now and then, too. Not very often. But it's kind of a—'' She broke off, seeming to search for the right term.

''Kind of a scientific stupor,'' Ash said from the doorway.

''Oh, aren't you the clever one?'' Andie said, shooting him an admonishing look.

''I'm the normal one. The average one,'' he said with emphasis as he strolled into the room. ''And I came to join the panic.''

Andie looked down her nose at him. ''We are not in a panic. We are organized and calm.''

Glory smiled at the teasing quality of their relationship, and felt a little pluck of yearning to be on the inside of such a relationship. It was almost as if they were brother and sister, and though Glory had a sister, unfortunately she'd never been close to her.

Ash switched his attention to Glory with a searching glance. ''How'd Caleb talk you into coming with him? He was in the doghouse when I left.''

Fighting a swift surge of embarrassment, Glory recalled the argument with Caleb. ''A misunderstanding,'' she said. ''And Caleb can be very—'' She paused, her diplomatic instincts failing her.

"Persuasive?" Andie offered doubtfully.

Ash snickered. "More like a pain in the butt."

"Persistent," Glory amended.

"How serious is it?" Ash probed.

"Don't snoop," Andie told him. "Glory's just gotten here and even though we're dying of curiosity, it's not fair to grill her about Caleb." She slid a glance to Glory. "Unless she wants to take pity on us and tell us on her own."

They were fun and endearing, and she felt a special warmth for them because of their obvious affection for Caleb, but her thoughts were still too tentative to share. She crossed her arms over her chest and took a step back. "Nothing's settled," she said. "We haven't been seeing each other that long, and Caleb's very busy with his research."

"But not too busy for you," Andie said, a hint of concern darkening her voice.

Glory opened her mouth, then closed it. "Not yet. Is there something I can do to help?"

A knowing glance crossed Andie's face as if she could tell Glory was uncomfortable. "Nothing right now. Make yourself at home and plan on going out with Samantha and me after the rehearsal dinner." She gave a conspiratorial smile. "We can compare notes on what it's like to be involved with genius research scientist types."

"Eli and Caleb will be thrilled," Ash interjected dryly. "Speaking of Eli," he said to Andie, "he asked me to come and get you. Some woman's at the door. He called her the barracuda."

Andie nodded. "I know who she is. C'mon. We'd

better give Glory a minute's peace, or she'll run away and we'll have to deal with Caleb's temper.''

A crazy mix of feelings fought for dominion inside Glory as she watched them leave her room. She turned back around and looked out the window at the green lawn. Although Andie had said she didn't want Glory to feel pressured, Glory did. Part of her quandary was whether Caleb would be able to tear himself away from his work enough to be concerned about a little child. His ease with Fletcher proved he possessed the capacity to genuinely care for a child.

Being around Caleb's family was another subtle point for his case. It would be easy to care for these people, tempting for them to care for her. She'd lost so many of her associations after her divorce, and Glory missed feeling connected to people.

Weary of the endless debate raging inside her, she was tempted to say yes and be done with it. He was temperamental, moody and pushy. But, God help her, she was in love with him, and she was sick of trying to deny it to herself.

It was strange. Her ex-husband had used the love words with well-worn regularity, but Glory had never felt a fraction of the passion or emotion from him she did from Caleb. Spending her life with Caleb, she suspected, would be like taking a ride on a roller coaster.

Glory had always been afraid of roller coasters.

Chapter Ten

"I want to marry her," Caleb said.

Ash choked on his beer. Eli just stared.

After spending the past hour at the local pub toasting the demise of Eli's bachelorhood and the beginning of his marriage, the conversation had begun to fade, and Ash had started needling Caleb about Glory. His patience shot, he finally said what was grating on him.

"I thought you weren't planning on anything permanent," Ash said.

"I wasn't," he said irritably.

"Have you asked her yet?" asked Eli.

He nodded. "She said no." He drummed his fingers on the wooden table. "Then she agreed to think about it."

Eli cocked his head to one side consideringly. "It took a while to persuade Andie," he admitted. "She'd been engaged to a jerk and was gun-shy."

"So, what'd you do?" Unaccustomed to spilling his guts to his brothers, Caleb felt as if the question was extricated from him like a sore tooth.

"I paid a lot of attention to her and kept after her." Eli grinned like a man who'd captured the prize. "It wasn't difficult to pay attention to her. It got to the point where being with her felt a lot more right than being without her."

Caleb's gut twisted. He identified with what Eli said about how being with a particular woman felt so right.

"Have you done the regular stuff like give her flowers and jewelry and tell her you love her?" Ash asked.

Caleb paused, mentally addressing each item on Ash's list. *No, no and no.* His brothers must have read his face.

Eli rubbed his forehead.

Ash rolled his eyes. "Well, hell, no wonder."

Caleb gritted his teeth. "I've pointed out every logical reason why we should get married, from sex to taxes, and she still just says she'll think about it."

Eli bit his lip, making a valiant effort not to laugh. "You're not really trying to use logic to win a woman, are you?"

Caleb wished he'd kept his mouth shut. "I've never been partial to Shakespeare, so I don't have anything else."

"If you're not in love with her, then maybe you shouldn't get married," Ash observed.

His mind instantly rebelled. "I want to marry her. I care about her," he said. "She's important to me, maybe the most important person in the world to me."

Eli rubbed his chin and nodded. "Do you think she's in love with you?"

Caleb thought about it for a moment and felt a flood of warmth steal over him. "Yeah. I think she is," he said gruffly.

"She might just need some time," Eli told him. "But I think most women want to hear that you love them."

They didn't have time. Glory was carrying his baby now. He couldn't explain it, but for a man who'd never given a rip for social conventions, he wanted a marriage certificate with his and Glory's names on the dotted line.

Signaling the scantily clad waitress for another round, Ash spoke with the authority of a man who'd maneuvered past the defenses of a number of women. "You're gonna have to cough up the words, Caleb."

The notion made him restless and uneasy. He shrugged to loosen the tension in his shoulders. "Glory knows it needs to be more than words. Her ex-husband was smooth. He had all the words, but he doesn't have her now."

A thoughtful silence descended on the three brothers. Eli cleared his throat. "Her ex-husband might not have her now," his brother said in a gentle voice, "but technically neither do you."

"Every now and then," Andie confessed over her strawberry daiquiri, "Eli gets totally focused on one thing, and I have to be extremely assertive to get his attention.''

"The verbal equivalent of knocking him upside the head,'' Samantha added, then looked at Glory. "I think you might have been a princess.''

Glory shared a conciliatory smile with Andie. Andie had a soft, gentle streak that appealed to her while Sam, she'd learned, was heavily into reincarnation and evaluated everyone she met in terms of their past lives. She'd also learned the two women had met because they were both nurses at the same hospital. Joining them had been fun, although she generally didn't frequent the type of establishment that featured shirtless male waiters serving drinks and dancing.

"And Caleb was a knight during the Crusades. A man with a mission,'' Sam murmured, and pointed her nearly empty glass in Glory's direction. "Not an easy man to love.''

She hadn't drunk anything alcoholic, but the late hour and easy company had loosened her tongue. "You're not telling me anything I don't know. I think that's what has me stalled. I wonder if he would be better off without . . . an encumbrance.''

"Maybe,'' Sam said, and tucked a dollar bill into the waistband of the man gyrating beside their table and gently waved him away. "Talented, but distracting,'' she murmured with a mischievous smile. "Shame he's not my type.''

"She tends to go for a high-achiever kind of man,'' Andie explained.

"It's a primitive need. I like the modern-day version of the good hunter and gatherer. A man who knows how to make money.''

"I noticed Ash was watching you at the rehearsal," Andie slyly pointed out.

"He can watch."

"He's a nice guy with a great body," Glory added, getting into the conversational play.

"I'll concede the great body, but as much as that tempts me, I don't think my destiny lies with a bricklayer."

"Snob," Andie said.

"Easy for you to say. You're marrying Mr. Brilliant, and Glory here is probably headed down the aisle with another Masters egghead."

"That's really not definite," Glory interjected, fighting a depressing sense of the inevitable. "As you said, he's a hard man to love."

"But you do love him, don't you?" Andie asked gently.

Glory held her breath. She'd never said it aloud. It was as if she kept it buried, then maybe it would go away. She looked at Andie, who was waiting expectantly, and sighed. "Yes," she admitted, "but I'm not sure marriage is the right . . ."

"Are you worried whether he's capable of being a husband or not?"

"That's part of it," she said, but she was also thinking of the baby.

Andie stirred her melted daiquiri. "This might sound strange, but since I met Caleb last year, I've always thought of him as a man with untapped potential."

"That's a nice way of putting it," Samantha said dryly.

Andie tossed her a dark look. "I mean it. Sure, he's brilliant, and he's dedicated to doing this important drug research. But you know, Caleb is more than his mission. He's a man, and it's going to take someone very special to remind him of that. The directors in his lab are interested in his brain, but they won't care about his heart until it affects his work."

Glory's chest tightened at Andie's words. It would be all too easy for Caleb to lose himself in his research again. Even she would have to admit that he seemed to want more, to need more. He wanted her. Maybe he needed her.

That sensation of riding a roller coaster rocked through her again, leaving her slightly nauseous. She took a quick breath and lifted her glass of ginger ale to Andie in a toast of admiration at her perceptiveness. "Eli's a lucky man," she said.

After a few more toasts, and a rather provocative dance performed by their waiter in Andie's honor, the three women went home.

Too restless to sleep, Glory stood staring out the window at the moon and stars. Wrapping her light robe around her, she leaned her head against the windowpane. She had left her door cracked for ventilation, and a much-needed breeze sifted through the window.

She heard a light tap at her door and turned to see Caleb. Her heart took a dip. Dressed in an unbuttoned shirt, jeans and no shoes, he looked as if he were fighting sleep, too. "Busy day," he murmured, moving toward her. "I thought you'd be asleep by now."

"Too much excitement, I guess," she said, and wondered why his mere presence always sent a thrill racing through her. "What about you?"

He stood next to her and shrugged. "My mind is on."

Glory looked up at him again and saw that he'd been raking his fingers through his hair. Wound tighter than a steel spring, he gazed at her with a combination of hunger and possessiveness that made her mouth dry.

She glanced away. "Makes you wish you had an On-Off switch sometimes."

He slipped his hand to her nape. "Yeah."

His gentle massage eased some of her tension. "You're good with Fletch."

"I understand him."

She closed her eyes and allowed him to pull her against him. "I like your brothers. I like Andie, too."

"That's good," he said, rubbing his chin against her hair.

Sensing he had something on his mind, she stifled a sigh. He wasn't being forthcoming. "Caleb, why'd you come here tonight?"

She felt his pause in measured heartbeats. "I'm not good with words. My verbal test scores bear out that fact," he finally muttered. "I'm probably never going to say exactly what you want to hear. But I need you to know you're important to me."

She tilted her head to look up at him. Her chest felt tight and achy. "Because of the baby?"

"Partly," he said. "The fact that you're carrying my child makes you different." He sifted his fingers through her hair. "But, Glory, you were different before the baby."

Her fear spilled out in a whisper. "How do you know you won't change your mind?"

He narrowed his eyes as he considered her question, then shook his head in frustration. "More words I don't have." He cupped her face in his hands and wrapped her in his green gaze. "There are laws of nature. Chemicals that no matter how often you combine them, one contains properties that compensate for the lack in the other. Hydrogen and oxygen make water. You put two basic elements together and the new combination is a miracle." He frowned. "What you do to me, it feels like a force of nature."

He lowered his mouth to hers and swore under his breath. "Not exactly Shakespeare."

Glory's eyes burned as he took her with a passionate kiss during which he tried to show what he couldn't say. She felt his every emotion—desire and tenderness, frustration and pain. Not exactly Shakespeare, he'd said and she agreed. Shakespeare had never made her feel this way.

"I now pronounce you man and wife. You may kiss the bride." The words were barely out of the minister's mouth before Eli took Andie into his arms, and the wedding guests applauded.

Feeling Caleb's gaze on her, Glory surreptitiously dabbed at her eyes with a crumpled tissue. Despite the brief time she'd known Eli and Andie, it was obvious they shared a special love. It showed in everything— the way he held her close to him when he didn't have to, the way she seemed to glow. Glory wondered if they had any idea how truly fortunate they were, to love and know they were loved in return.

A few vague memories of her own wedding passed through her mind. Young, nervous and so overwhelmed that Senator Richard Danson had chosen *her,* she hadn't had a clue what was in store for her.

During the exchange of vows, Caleb had watched her the entire time as if he was ready to make his promises today. His expression tied her in knots and filled her with longing. He might as well put his intentions on a platter for the world to see.

She hadn't slept well last night. It was becoming increasingly difficult to sustain this emotional limbo with Caleb. His tension was palpable, and the stress was killing her appetite. She'd eaten only a little breakfast and skipped lunch completely.

At the reception Glory tried to put aside her confusion for the sake of the celebration. The serving tables groaned under the huge selection of food, but, oddly enough, the aroma bothered her.

"You look a little pale," Sam said. "What happened? Did your knight forget his chivalry?"

Glory laughed despite the disconcerting edge of nausea creeping in. "I don't think chivalry is a high priority with Caleb, but he has gone to get me some punch." Her stomach turned again, making her revise her plans. She took a slow breath. "To tell you the truth, I think I could use a trip to the ladies' room. Do you know where it is?"

"I'll go with you," Sam said, turning to lead the way down the hall of the quaint hotel. "I want to freshen my lipstick. Andie looks gorgeous, doesn't she?"

"Yes, she does," Glory agreed, not wanting to draw attention to herself. She followed Sam into the powder room, immediately searching for privacy.

Sam paused in front of the mirror and sighed. "It's almost enough to make a girl believe in happily ever after. Did you see—"

"Excuse me," Glory mumbled, and bolted for a vacant stall.

After she came back out, Sam, her eyes wide with concern, appeared at her side with a cool, damp paper towel. "I was rattling off a mile a minute. Why didn't you say you felt sick?"

Still feeling weak, Glory shook her head and leaned against the wall. "I just felt a little queasy and I thought it would pass, but it didn't."

Samantha frowned, and Glory could practically see her put on her nurse's cap. She put a hand to Glory's forehead. "You think it's a virus? You don't feel like you have a fever."

Glory tried to steady herself, and took slow deep breaths. "It's not a virus. I didn't have anything for lunch." She stalled, wondering how to get through this situation. She really didn't feel up to going back out there to face the crowd and those tables of food. "Do you think they might have some saltines?"

Samantha paused for a long moment, then realization crossed her face. "When are you due?"

"Not until March. Nobody knows," she added, realizing with a sinking sensation that everything was about to change. She'd wanted a little more time to get used to the idea that she was pregnant, to find a little peace, to decide what she was going to do about Caleb.

"Does Caleb?"

Her heart twisted painfully. "That's why he wants me to marry him."

Sam gave her a long look full of frustration and sympathy. "Oh, hell."

"Yes," she agreed, and closed her eyes as the queasiness rose again. "I thought morning sickness was just for mornings."

Sam smothered a chuckle. "That's a common fallacy. Nausea in pregnancy can occur anytime during the day."

That fun fact failed to comfort Glory. "If I see food again, I'm going to embarrass myself."

"Do you want to go home?"

Glory stifled a moan. This was not how she'd pictured announcing her pregnancy. She'd hoped for something more discreet and dignified. Losing her cookies at a wedding reception didn't appeal to her. "I think I'll just stand here for a—"

"Excuse me," an elderly woman said as she approached. "There's a nice young man outside who's looking for someone named Glory."

Desperation raced through her. "Oh, Lord. You tell him if he comes in here, I'll never speak to him again," she said with as much force as she could muster. "I mean it."

Sam looked perplexed. "Even Caleb wouldn't barge into a—"

"Oh, yes, he would!" She shook her head. "Tell him— Tell him to go find some crackers or something. He does better when he has a job to do." Her mind whirling with the same force as her stomach, she felt something inside her crumble. A flimsy barrier she'd erected to stay off the roller coaster. "And tell him," she added quietly, bowing to the inevitable as she turned back to the stall, "I said yes."

"Get some crackers," Samantha told Caleb in a no-nonsense voice.

He craned to see past her. "Okay, but—"

"She said she'll never speak to you again if you go in there," she said flatly.

He felt his shoulder muscles clench and swore under his breath. "I've got to know if she's okay."

Samantha's expression softened just barely. "She's pregnant, Caleb. Her hormones are in a rage, and she's currently experiencing one of the joys of pregnancy. Nausea."

He stared at her in disbelief. "She told you?"

"I guessed."

"Oh." He raked his hand through his hair and battled down a feeling of helplessness.

"You need to get those crackers," she reminded him.

Caleb nodded. "Yeah. Right." He took a deep breath to alleviate the sudden weight of responsibility he felt. He'd known Glory was pregnant, but this made it seem more real. He turned down the hall. "I'll go and—"

"Oh, she said one other thing," Samantha added almost as an afterthought.

Caleb glanced back at her. "What?"

"She said yes."

His heart stuttered. "Yes," he echoed, demanding confirmation.

"That's what she said," Samantha replied with a tinge of impatience. "Yes."

Caleb walked unseeingly down the hall, mentally moving Glory into his house, mentally getting a marriage license, mentally gaining a *wife*. After all his persistence, the prospect nearly knocked him flat on his face.

Caleb willed the anger down the best that he could, moving Glory out by force. Finally, they walked to their car. Quietly, tense, Caleb drove to the place he had reserved for himself at a bed-and-breakfast on the...

Chapter Eleven

They married less than one week later in a civil ceremony at the courthouse. Eli and Andie tried to talk Caleb into waiting so they could have a more elaborate ceremony, but Caleb wanted it done.

Neither of their families was able to attend. Eli and Andie were on their honeymoon, and Ash was committed to staying in Cary to take care of Fletch. Glory's parents were on a cruise. Her sister sent silver candlesticks.

Her blue eyes serious, her smiles sparse, Glory wore a pink feminine dress and clenched the bouquet he'd bought her in her hands as the justice of the peace conducted the brief ceremony. Her hand was cold and she looked scared.

Caleb couldn't take his eyes off her. Up until the

moment she said, "I do," he wondered if Glory would back out.

"I do," she finally said, and Caleb felt the impact of her promise clear to his bones.

The justice of the peace pronounced them man and wife and Caleb thanked God he could finally take her into his arms. He kissed her thoroughly, determined to wipe out every bit of fear, every doubt. He kissed her until she was clinging to his shoulders.

When he drew back, he watched her blink to regain her equilibrium. "Okay?" he murmured, his hands still wrapped around her waist.

"Ask me in a minute," she said, and something inside him eased.

After the two clerical workers who'd served as witnesses congratulated them, Caleb took Glory's hand and led her outside the courthouse. Squinting his eyes against the bright July sun, he looked at her. She still seemed a little dazed.

"That was fast," she said numbly.

His lips twisted. "I wondered if you would back out."

"There wasn't time."

His heart clenched and he stared at her. "Did you want to?"

She met his gaze and shook her head. "No. But I didn't expect to feel so nervous."

Caleb squeezed her hand. "You and me both. It took me four times to tie my tie this morning."

She laughed. "How many times does it usually take?"

Caleb hesitated, then grinned at her joke. "Three, Mrs. Smarty-pants. Now let me take my bride to lunch."

He followed his list to the letter. Ash had called and bent his ear with tips on how to handle a new bride. Despite Ash's lack of experience in matrimonial matters, Caleb had not only listened, he'd taken notes. Ash had emphasized the fact that most men considered the chase over after the wedding. Since Glory had been pushed into marriage, Caleb had a tough road in front of him. The words of wisdom didn't comfort Caleb one bit.

After lunch at a posh downtown restaurant, he drove to a popular honeymoon resort in Pennsylvania. While Glory took a bath in the heart-shaped bathtub surrounded by mirrors, he prowled around the room, tugging loose his tie and ditching his jacket. Every time he pictured Glory naked and wet in that decadent bathroom, he groaned. Pushing the erotic image from his mind, he adjusted the thermostat, turned on an FM radio station and ordered room service. Dinner, flowers and chilled champagne arrived within minutes.

After what seemed like an eternity, she came out of the bathroom wearing a long satin robe that emphasized her bottomless blue eyes and dark, tousled hair.

Caleb's heart stopped. Here was his bride.

"Hi," she said, meeting his gaze with a soft smile, then she glanced at the flowers. "What's all this? They're beautiful." Delighted, she bent to smell a rosebud. "How did you arrange it so quickly?"

He shrugged his shoulders, resolving to make use of a list more often. "The concierge was very cooperative."

"Yes, but someone had to give him instructions." She walked toward him, calm and confident, as if she didn't have a clue how she affected him. Stopping just inches away, she rose on tiptoe and brushed a quick kiss on his mouth. "Thank you."

That brief touch scorched him. Caleb shoved his hands into his pockets to keep from reaching for her.

She looked at him and her eyebrows furrowed in concern. "You seem a little tense. Is something wrong?"

He paused. "I'm not exactly sure what to do with a wife."

Uncertainty shadowed her eyes and she backed away. "I was afraid—"

Immediately realizing he'd said the wrong thing, Caleb closed his hands around her arms. "Don't be. It's been a long time since we've been together. I'm having a tough time keeping my hands off you, Glory."

Her eyes flashed. "Then why are you?"

Confused, he stared at her. "Why am I what?"

"Keeping your hands off me."

Caleb sucked in a quick breath of air. "I'm trying not to jump you," he said, eliminating any misunderstanding.

"Oh." She looked at him blankly for a long moment, then took him off guard by stepping closer and hugging him. Her sigh drifted against his chest. "This is going to take some work. You understanding me. Me understanding you."

Caleb wondered when he would get used to having her close, all the time. "Yeah."

"Think we're gonna be able to do it?"

"Yeah. If you promise to let me watch next time you take a bath in that bathroom."

He felt her smile against his chest. "Why didn't you just barge in and join me?"

"I thought about it. Long and hard," he added meaningfully.

She looked up at him and laughed. Her gaze meshed with his, her emotions shifting on her face like sand. Her smile faded and she threaded her fingers through his, rubbing her thumb over the golden band on his third finger. "I really want this to work."

"It will," he said. Another promise he didn't know how to keep. He just knew he would.

He could take her now, he realized, reading love and fear on her face. The fear ripped at him. He could wipe it away. Skip the dinner waiting on the table, and make love instead. The need to claim gnawed at him, but making love to Glory this time meant more. He'd been rushing her since they'd met again. Rushing her into bed with him. Rushing her into marriage. Tonight he didn't want to rush her. He wanted her satisfied in every sense of the word, so he lowered his mouth to hers for just a taste.

Opening to him, she slipped closer and curled her arms around his waist. She held him tight, as if she didn't want to let go, as if she was where she wanted to be, and it made Caleb's chest hurt. *Closer, pull me closer.*

Disturbed by the force of his need, he pulled back slowly. "Dinner first," he muttered, feeling her curious gaze on him. Turning away from her, he felt relief combined with the damnedest sense of loss. Shaking it off, he lifted the bottle of champagne. "Ready for a toast?"

"I really shouldn't. The doctor said it's best to avoid alcohol."

Caleb paused. "Well, hell."

Glory bit back a smile at his confounded expression. "It's okay. I can do without alcohol. It's the caffeine withdrawal that's killing me."

"I forgot about all that," he said, pulling out her chair. "Have you been sick anymore?"

"A couple of times," she admitted, joining him at the table. She did not admit, however, that her stomach wasn't feeling terrific at this very moment. Her wedding ceremony might not have lasted more than five minutes, but she was determined to have a wedding night to remember. She eyed the beef with doubt, and mentally whispered a prayer of thanks for the bread.

"How long does it usually last?" he asked, cutting into his rare steak.

Glory looked away. "A few hours." She didn't want to discuss her afternoon morning sickness. "This is a little premature, but have you thought about names?"

Caleb blinked. "Names?"

"For the baby." She washed down the bread with ice water, and reached for another roll. She didn't feel ready for the asparagus.

"We don't know if it's a girl or boy."

"I know. That's part of the fun." When he didn't seem to understand, she elaborated. "Guessing the sex and making up names. I'm not really into juniors, but if we had a boy, I thought it would be nice to give him the same middle name you have.''

"Okay," he said, as if she were picking out chewing gum flavor rather than his child's name.

Okay. As far as Caleb was concerned, it was settled. So much for the fun, she thought wryly. Maybe he would be more interested later. "The doctor also mentioned the prepared childbirth classes, but we won't have to worry about them until January or February." An unsettling thought occurred to her. "You *do* want to be there for the birth, don't you?"

"Yes. When are you moving into my house?"

Glory's gaze collided with his and she felt a ripple of anticipation race through her. *Sex.* The reason Caleb wasn't particularly interested in discussing baby names and childbirth classes was that he wanted to make love to her. And he wanted to do it now. She took a deep breath and prayed the rolling sensation in her stomach would subside. "I hadn't really decided. We've got to figure out what to do with my furniture."

"But there's no reason for you to sleep at your house anymore, is there?"

"No."

He covered her hand with his. "I want you in my bed from now on."

Her heart raced. Glory wondered how she could feel aroused and nauseated at the same time. He slid his finger between hers, rubbing gently, sensuously. He stroked her palm, the inside of her wrist, and the caress was oddly provocative.

She instinctively closed her hand around his finger, and the visual image of their coupled hands brought a more intimate union to mind. His hardness thrusting inside her softer, yielding flesh.

She risked a glance at Caleb and by the blatant desire written on his face, she knew he shared the same thoughts. Holding her gaze, he deliberately pressed his finger deeper into the crevice she'd created with her hand. His nostrils flared. "There's dessert if you want."

Glory swallowed hard. A knot of arousal warred with her increasing queasiness. "I couldn't eat it."

He lifted her hand to his mouth and kissed it. "I want you," he said, tugging her from her chair to his lap. "I've wanted you every night since I first had you."

He took her mouth in a frankly sexual kiss, using his tongue and teeth. Her body responded instantly. Her nipples drew into tight beads, and she felt a rush of heat. She couldn't resist his uninhibited desire for her. It made her feel so feminine, so necessary.

Everything else in their relationship might be complicated, but Caleb made this so easy. He wanted her with a power that made her tremble. She felt the pressure of his hardness against her thigh and was ready for everything he would give and take.

His passion almost overrode her rapidly rising queasiness. But her stomach rolled one time too many and she had to tear away from him. *Oh, no!*

Distressed, she shot a quick glance at his confused face and whispered, "I'm sorry. Really. I'm so sorry." Scrambling off his lap, she ran to the bathroom and surrendered to morning sickness at the inconvenient hour of 8:00 p.m. on her wedding night.

Forty-five minutes later Caleb stood outside the bathroom door with a box of saltine crackers and a glass of decaffeinated cola he'd ordered from room service. When he had been told the hotel restaurant didn't carry decaffeinated cola, he'd offered the waiter a twenty-dollar tip to find some. The two-liter plastic bottle now occupied the sterling silver champagne ice bucket.

"Are you sure you don't want to call your doctor?" he asked for the third time. Seeing her sick made him nervous.

"No," she said for the third time. He heard the sound of running water and her brushing her teeth. "I think I'll be okay if I lie down with a cool washcloth." She opened the door slightly. "Please tell me the food is gone."

The pleading note in her voice grabbed at him. "Room service has taken it away," he assured her.

She finally came out, still looking a little green around the gills and pressing a washcloth against her forehead. "I am so sorry, Caleb. This is terrible—"

"Stop," he told her, relieved to take control after feeling useless for the past forty-five minutes. "Do you want a drink?"

She sighed. "A little," she said, and took a tiny sip.

He set the drink and crackers on the nightstand, then put his arm around her. "Come to bed."

She didn't put up a fight, just let her satin robe slide to the floor and collapsed on the mattress. She was an incongruous sight with that mouth-watering satin gown shimmering over every curve with tempting ease, juxtaposed against the white cotton washcloth cover-

ing her eyes and forehead. "I'm sorry," she said
again. "You don't know how sorry."

"You mean because when I was getting ready to
make love to you, you ran for the john. If I were the
sensitive type, my ego would be crushed."

She lifted the corner of her washcloth to throw him
a caustic look with one eye, then weakly flapped her
hand at him. "I'll punch you for that in the morning."

Pleased at her improved response, he flipped the
washcloth over for her, putting the cooler side on her
forehead. "I'm sorry, too," he said in a low voice.
"Sorry you feel so damn rotten."

"Thanks for understanding." Her lips lifted in a
faint smile and she reached for his hand. "Not every
man would."

"My libido's strong enough to survive the hit," he
assured her. "I'll let you make it up to me."

She pinched him. A very un-Glorylike move.

Caleb muffled a chuckle and watched her until she
went to sleep. He turned out most of the lights, then
watched her some more. She looked small and vulnerable in her sleep. A strange feeling of tenderness
squeezed his heart. It bothered him. If it was this hard
to care for a person, he wondered what it was like to
be in love.

Glory woke early the next morning. Rain splat-
tered rhythmically against the window. She tried to go
back to sleep, but her stomach kept growling. Catch-
ing sight of the box of crackers on her nightstand, she
carefully got out of bed and took them with her to a
chair on the other side of the suite.

Feet curled beneath her, she devoured half of one waxed-paper-wrapped package, then drank a glass of water. All the while she watched Caleb. All the while he slept.

Arms outstretched, he lay sprawled on the bed as if he were unaccustomed to sharing his sleep space. The sheet had been kicked down to his knees, baring his chest and broad shoulders, baring his abdomen and powerful thighs, baring everything except what a pair of white briefs covered. She wondered if he usually slept nude.

The image brought a surprising rush of heat, an unexpected longing.

Rising, she walked to the side of the bed and gazed down at him. His eyebrows tugged down slightly as if he were frowning and Glory was filled with questions about this man she'd married, this man she really didn't know well at all.

What was he dreaming that left that dissatisfied expression on his face? Did he regret getting married? A lump formed in her throat. That was her greatest fear. She'd resigned herself to the fact that Caleb might never *love* her the way she'd always hoped to be loved, but she didn't think she could bear it if he regretted their marriage.

She reached out her hand to touch the frown line between his brows, but stopped just before she reached him, not quite prepared to deal with Caleb awake. She'd learned that dealing with a genius required planning. Flying by the seat of her pants didn't cut it.

Her gaze drifted over his body again. For such a cerebral man he was incredibly physical. The combination always caught her by surprise, but didn't displease her. It amazed her that although she had been married for five years, he seemed much more at ease with his sexual needs than she was with hers.

She frowned, digging her toes into the plush carpet. Maybe it was time for that to change. Maybe it was time for her to stop using the past as a guide for how she acted today. She pondered that for a moment, then went to the bathroom to freshen up.

"Good morning."

Caleb instantly recognized the silky whisper at his ear and felt himself lured to the land of the living. He breathed in her scent when a soft strand of hair skimmed over his neck. Never at his best in the morning, he worked his heavy eyelids. Soothing fingertips slipped over his forehead and he sighed. The gentle touch could have eased him back to sleep if she hadn't chosen that moment to shift her body so that he felt her breasts encased in slippery satin against his ribs.

His hands instinctively sought the curve of her waist to draw her closer and he looked at her through hooded eyes. Her brushed hair hung in silky waves to her shoulders, and her gaze was curious. If he didn't know better, he'd say *sexually* curious. "Are you better?"

Her lips tilted in a sensuous grin. "Much. How about you?"

"I'm—" He broke off when she began to draw circles on his chest with her fingers. Feeling an instant surge of heat, he cleared his throat. "You've been awake for a while, haven't you?"

She nodded and dipped her head to brush a kiss on his chest. "I ate some crackers, but I'm still going to want breakfast."

Ignoring his rapid arousal, he asked, "You want to call room service?"

Her mouth still on his chest, she lifted her gaze to meet his. "Not yet." She paused a full thumping heartbeat. "What do you want?"

Caleb swore under his breath. "No big mystery there," he muttered, and pulled her on top of him. The texture of cool satin outlining her curves brushing over his skin made him groan. He slid perfectly between her thighs and shifted. They both heard the crackle of paper at the same time.

Glory frowned. "What was that?" Slipping one of her hands from him, she searched between them and found a crumpled piece of paper with his handwriting on it.

She looked at the paper and shot him a softly accusing look. "You were in bed with me last night and you were writing chemistry formulas."

"You were asleep," he said, hoping like hell she wasn't as offended as she sounded. "There was a pad of paper and a pen on the nightstand. It's a habit," he said helplessly.

"A man with a mission. A hard man to love," she muttered, more to herself than to him. "Is this going to change the course of human history?" she asked about the formula on the paper.

"No."

She crumpled the paper and tossed it over the edge of the bed, then met his gaze with a determined, wholly feminine expression. "You have your mission in life. I think mine is to eradicate these papers from our bed.''

"You misunderstand. I—''

"I know,'' she interrupted. "There's a lot about you I don't understand. There's a lot I want to know, but right now I want a different kind of chemistry lesson from Caleb Masters.'' She pointed her fingertip at his chest. "I want to know what turns you on.''

Caleb's heart pounded. "You,'' he said in a voice that sounded rough to his own ears.

She shifted back in place so that his hardness rubbed against the heat between her thighs. "You're going to have to be more specific.''

He thrust against her, the layers of cotton and satin tempting and frustrating him. "I want you to kiss me,'' he muttered.

"Where?''

He drew in a quick breath of air filled with her scent, and his frustration mounted. "Hell, my mouth, my neck, every—''

He broke off when her mouth covered his, sweet and searching. She bit gently at his lip and tugged, then replaced her teeth with her tongue. Restless, Caleb rubbed his hands down her satin-covered back and cupped her rear end. She undulated against him and he was cursing the guy who'd invented underwear.

"What now?'' she whispered next to his ear, and sent a shower of electricity through his nerve endings.

He tugged at the waistband of his briefs, but her hands replaced his. Watching him, she removed them, then started on her nightgown.

"Wait. That gown—''

She paused, lifting her eyebrows. Then as if she'd read his fantasy, a knowing expression came over her face. "You want me to keep it on," she said, leaning against him. "You like the way it feels."

"Yeah." He pushed down the straps to reveal her breasts, and the sight made him pulse in every erogenous zone at once. Touching her peaked rose nipples, he felt her arch against him. The movement stroked his erection, titillated his mind. She made him hungry and crazy, and damn if he didn't keep coming back for more.

Lifting her, he took her tender areola in his mouth and sucked because he wanted to taste her, because he wanted every intimacy. He knew she was sensitive there and he wanted her as hungry as he was.

She gasped, her eyes fluttering in pleasure. "You're making it hard for me to remember my mission."

"Watching you is part of the turn-on," he told her when she shivered. He put his hands beneath the long gown, dragging it up the length of her thighs. When he continued to encounter bare skin all the way up to her waist, he started to sweat. "You're not wearing anything underneath this."

She drew her legs on either side of his and leaned back so that she sat in his lap. Her eyes were soft, dark with arousal. "You don't like that?"

Acutely sensitive to the satin that separated his flesh from hers, he clenched his jaw. "Yes, but, hell—"

"Then why are you swearing?" She scooted farther down his thighs, and with an expression of teasing curiosity that nearly undid him, she folded the corner of her gown around her hand like a glove and enclosed his shaft.

Caleb went through the roof. He closed his eyes because the erotic sight of her sitting bare breasted on his thighs combined with the sensation of her satin-wrapped hand around him was enough to make him climax. When she started to stroke him, he began to swear. His body trembling, he reached for her and turned her beneath him.

Staring into her eyes, he heaved several deep breaths. His mouth was so dry he could barely speak. "My turn," he managed to choke out. His passion driving him, he cupped her heat and rubbed her intimately with the satin nightgown. He caught her moan with his mouth and fondled her sensitive femininity.

Once a delicious seduction, the satin became a barrier. He pushed it aside and felt her warm and wet with his hands, then his mouth.

"Caleb," she protested, pushing at his shoulders.

"You wanted to know what turns me on," he told her low and deep. He stroked the insides of her thighs and met her hesitant gaze. "Let me take you this way."

She bit her lip and held on. Her fingernails digging into his shoulders, she whimpered breathlessly, writhing beneath him. *Closer, let me closer.* The words played in his mind like a chant. Aroused but feeling so much more than physical pleasure, he couldn't begin to comprehend it all. He only knew he needed everything with her. He needed the sweet taste of her, the sensation of her body arching in pleasure, the sound of his name on her lips. He needed to claim her this way, every way.

She stiffened and cried out. Rocking with the force of her climax, she looked as if she were shattering.

Overwhelmed by a feeling of protectiveness, he held her tightly against him.

Her obvious vulnerability alarmed him. "It's okay," he murmured. "It's okay."

"I wanted you with me," she said breathlessly.

Her words struck his heart and made him throb. Caleb understood and shifted between her legs, plunging inside her hot, wet entrance in one stroke.

He swore.

She sighed.

She wove her fingers between his and arched, bringing him deeper. With just a tilt of her pelvis, she made his head spin.

"I love you," she whispered, the message written on her face, demonstrated in her body.

He thrust again, and her countermovements clawed at him with pleasure and pain. She was so tight. She was so *his*.

It was hard to watch. It was hard to feel this much, but Caleb made himself, and she took him over the edge.

Chapter Twelve

Glory was sick again that night.

In fact, she was sick every night for the next four weeks. For the sake of survival, she developed a pattern of going to work early, leaving early, preparing a simple dinner, then going to bed.

She could tell Caleb was bemused by her behavior, but she didn't see any way around it until the nausea passed. And, God help her, she hoped it passed soon.

Emotionally, she was as changeable as the wind. One minute she was certain everything would be fine with her and Caleb and the baby. She was confident in their future. Her love and Caleb's determination would get them through. An hour later doubts would swarm around her. Unfortunately, since her resistance was down, she couldn't always push them aside when she needed to.

Prone to tears, she did her best to hide them from Caleb, but he came home late one evening and caught her crying in bed. Shoving his hands into his pockets, he gazed down at her, rumpled from a long day at work. "What happened?"

"Nothing, really," she said, feeling ridiculous, but unable to control it. She blew her nose. "I guess I'm just tired. Tired of being sick. I come home, fix dinner and most of the time I don't even eat it. By the time you get home, all we do is say hello, then I go upstairs. It's like we're not even married," she murmured, surprised she'd let that last line spill out. She was usually careful what she said to him.

His eyes were dark and intent. "If you're fixing dinner just for me, stop."

Her chest tightened. "No," she wailed, sitting up and feeling the customary lurch in her stomach. Her emotions had been bottled up too long. "Then I'll feel totally unnecessary."

"Unnecessary," he repeated, his eyebrows wrinkling in confusion.

"We don't talk. We don't make love," she said in a low, uneven voice, and glanced away. "The least I can do is fix one meal."

He sat down on the bed next to her, appearing completely confounded. "Do you want to make love?"

Yes. When they made love, they had no communication problems. She bit her lip. "Not now. I can't at night, but you're not a morning person—"

"I can adjust," he told her in a rough voice that affected her like a caress.

Glory stared at him and blinked at the burning sensation in her eyes. Lord, she'd missed him. "I feel useless."

Caleb's lips twisted. "I thought I was the only one."

"Why? I'm the one who comes home and goes straight to bed." She shook her head. "I've never worried so much in my life. I worry about the baby. I worry about you. I—"

Caleb stopped her with one touch of his hand. "You're worried about me?"

Uncomfortable with what she'd already disclosed, she looked away again. "I don't know. I know you work late downstairs every night and I'm afraid you're going to turn back into a research machine." She didn't speak her greater fear that he would regret marrying her. She simply couldn't.

"Is this a gender thing?" he asked in a hesitant voice.

"A pregnancy thing," she told him, feeling the slightest bit of amusement at his completely baffled expression. "Hormone flux."

He nodded soberly. "Does it last the entire nine months?" He was clearly trying to keep the note of dread from his tone.

"The second trimester is supposed to be much better."

He nodded, sighing in relief. "So this is temporary."

Her heart welling with love for him, she wrapped her arms around him, wanting to feel his strength and warmth. "I've really missed you."

"We've seen each other every day," he said logically, yet pulled her closer.

Glory stifled a sigh. He just didn't understand.

As if he was determined to make sure she felt married, Caleb began to make love to her in the morning, every morning. For a non-morning person, he was extremely adept at drawing out her body's secrets. She was always amazed at how a sleepy seduction could turn into a mating that had them both crying out. The passion and closeness they shared helped balance her mood swings.

The following week, however, he missed her doctor's appointment. After sitting in the waiting room and glancing up every time the door opened, Glory finally gave up and went to the examination room.

When the doctor placed the special stethoscope on her abdomen, she listened to the rapid swishing sound of her baby's heartbeat and wished Caleb was there to hear it, too, to share the sense of wonder. Instead, he'd probably gotten tied up with something at the lab.

Struggling to keep perspective, she wondered if it would always be this way with him. Torn between hurt and frustration, she spent the drive home rehearsing what she would say to him.

Caleb arrived home late and was surprised to find Glory waiting for him in the den. She was usually upstairs battling nausea while he made sure she had an adequate supply of tea and crackers. Whenever he looked at the dark circles under her eyes, he was filled with an inexplicable yet very masculine sense of guilt. She wouldn't be nauseated if he hadn't gotten her pregnant. The darker, ruthless side of him pointed out she wouldn't be wearing his ring, either, and he was damn glad Glory was living under his roof as his wife.

"You're not sick," he said, pleased to see the color in her face.

"No, this was a pretty good day." She glanced at him with an inquiring gaze that was a shade cooler than usual. "How was your day?"

The customary words never failed to soothe him at the end of his worst days, but today he felt a trickle of uneasiness. He couldn't put his finger on it, but there was something strange about her tone. He sat in the chair across from her. "Busy as hell. We received some new equipment and had to work the bugs out of it. That's why I'm late."

She nodded. "And did you get the bugs out of it?"

Too polite. "Yes."

She took a measured breath. "Well, I guess our marriage has something in common with your lab. We need to work the bugs out of it." She folded her hands. "I realize you're very busy, and that your research is important, but in the future if you aren't able to meet me at a time we've agreed upon, I would appreciate a phone call."

Caleb frowned. She was using that supercalm PR tone, and he had an ugly suspicion she was upset as hell. "What are you talking about?"

Hurt and anger sliced across her face, then she quickly covered it and looked away. "It's not that big of a deal," she said as if she were trying to convince herself. "It was just a routine doctor appointment, but you said you wanted—"

"Oh, hell." Recalling the doctor appointment he'd promised he wanted to attend, Caleb raked his hand through his hair and stood.

Clearly ruffled and trying not to show it, Glory stood, too, and gave a stiff shrug. "In the overall scheme of things, it may not seem that important to you, but I think I'll operate better if I know whether you're actually going to..."

Caleb reached for her shoulders. "I'm sorry."

Suddenly silent, she met his gaze, and Caleb knew he'd hurt her.

He swore again. "It was a jerk thing to do."

"Yes, it was."

Caleb winced at her quick, soft agreement.

After a long moment where she seemed to measure his sincerity, he felt some of the tension leave her body. Her lips lifted in a secret smile. "I heard our baby's heartbeat."

A never-before-felt thrill bucked through his bloodstream. *Our baby.* He squeezed her shoulders. "What did it sound like? How fast was it? What kind of—"

Glory covered his mouth and laughed. "Stop. It was a sweeping sound. Fast, really fast," she said. "A hundred and fifty beats a minute. Dr. Hill said it sounded strong."

Seeing the wonder and excitement in her eyes grabbed at his gut. He shook his head. "Damn, I wish I'd been there. I wanted to ask her if the combination in your multivitamin is the optimal one."

Her eyes widened in surprise. "I didn't know you'd even noticed my vitamins."

"I read the label one night when you were asleep." It had been a night he'd been overwhelmed at the prospect of fatherhood, at the reality of having a wife and still not knowing what to do with her. Uncomfortable with the memory, he went on. "What else did she do?"

Glory shrugged. "It was a routine visit. Blood pressure, weight gain, that sort of—"

"So what was it?"

"My blood pressure was normal."

"And your weight?" he prompted.

She hesitated. "I lost a little, but that's not unusual during the first trimester."

Caleb frowned. "You're going to have to eat more."

"I will," she assured him, backing away and grimacing. "When I can keep more down."

"Aren't pregnant women supposed to have cravings?"

"I guess some do," she said uncertainly. "But the closest thing I have to a craving right now is saltine crackers." She shot him a wary glance. "Are you going to grill me like this every time I go to the doctor?"

"I prefer to think of it as gaining information."

She looked at him in disbelief. "I never thought I'd see the day." She pointed at him. "You just tried to pull a PR trick on me. Restating a negative as a positive."

Caleb laughed at her perplexed expression, closed his hand around her finger and tugged her into his arms. "You asked a question, I answered it."

"Yes, but—"

He lowered his mouth a breath away from hers. "I'm a scientist. I need information." He hesitated and spoke from somewhere inside him, somewhere that seemed to belong only to Glory. "I'm your husband. I need to know you're okay."

She looked at him with a barely concealed longing in her eyes that cut at him. She wanted more from him, and Caleb feared he didn't have it to give.

Glory's nausea finally passed, and before she realized it, it was November, she was showing and she was filled with a burning drive to get the nursery ready. Pleased if not totally secure with her relationship with Caleb, she was always thinking of ways to get him to open up. Samantha had been right when she'd said he wasn't an easy man to love. Glory had accepted the fact, however, that the choice to love Caleb was out of her hands. She loved him, and living with him had made her love grow deeper and fuller.

Loving him, however, didn't mean she understood him. She could tell it was difficult for him to tear his mind from his research, and she didn't resent him, because the poor man was obviously trying to do his best. But he was still a mystery to her in many ways. It didn't make sense, but sometimes, after they made love, he looked at her with an odd tinge of fear in his eyes. She hadn't found the nerve to ask him why, but she thought about it often.

"Not today, though," she said resolutely to Fancy, who sat in the patch of waning sunlight in front of the window. "Today it's me and Sting and baby."

Fancy just yawned in response. With Sting urging her on from her CD player, Glory stirred the paint. Mindful of her balance, she braced herself on the stepladder and rolled another coat of lemon meringue paint on the wall.

"What in *hell* are you doing?"

Her heart leaping, Glory jumped and teetered off-balance. She caught a quick glance of Caleb running toward her before the ladder shifted and the paint pan tilted. *The baby. The baby. The baby.* Panic crowded her chest. She dropped the roller, and Caleb was reaching for her.

Solid and strong beneath her, he held her tightly, swearing under his breath. She clung to him for a moment, then pushed away from him in frustration. "Don't do that! You scared me."

"I scared *you?*" He glared at her, emotion glinting from his green eyes. "What do you think you're doing?"

"Painting the nursery lemon meringue like I told you." Breathless, she clenched her damp, trembling palms into fists. "And I was fine before you yelled at me."

He jerked his hand through his hair in agitation. "You couldn't have told me you planned to paint today. There's no way I would have permitted it."

His statement hung between them for a timeless moment. Glory stared at him. *"Permitted it?"*

Caleb's nostrils flared as if he were taking a deep breath to calm himself, and Glory could practically feel the heat wave rolling off him. "I don't want you on that damn ladder. It's not safe."

"I was being very careful."

"You almost fell." He sounded as if he were ready to chew glass.

"When you yelled at me," Glory reminded him, then stopped. This had gotten completely out of control. The man could obliterate years of assertiveness training in thirty seconds flat. It was tough going head-to-head with Caleb when she was dressed in paint-covered gym shorts and one of his T-shirts, and her hair was pulled back in a ponytail.

Irritated, she walked toward the CD player to turn down the volume. "Maybe you were zoned out on one of your chemical formulas or something, but I told you I was going to paint—"

"When?"

Glory hesitated and thought about it. "This morning after—"

"We made love." He looked up at the ceiling as if he were searching for help. "The only thing I remember is something about lemon meringue, and that's because it inspired all kinds of creative thoughts in conjunction with your breasts." He met her gaze meaningfully. "And, yes, I've noticed that your breasts are fuller than before."

Blunt again. Glory willed herself not to blush. After all, the man knew every inch of her body. "The paint color is lemon meringue," she said, firmly bringing the discussion under control. "And I want to do a wallpaper border with ducks and bunnies."

Caleb was quiet for a long moment. His mouth twitched. "Ducks and bunnies?"

"Yes," she said, standing toe-to-toe with his assaulted sense of masculinity. "Did you have a different suggestion appropriate for a baby?"

"What if it's a boy?"

"Boy babies like ducks and bunnies," she told him, picking up the paint roller. She was glad she'd put plastic and newspaper on the floor. "I thought we'd save the footballs and airplanes for later."

Caleb went to her side as she knelt to get the paint pan. He swore. "Why are you doing all this? You're pregnant. You're supposed to be taking it easy."

Glory saw the frustration on his face and felt a burst of affection mixed with amusement. He cared, she realized, more than he'd probably planned. The knowledge thrilled her and fed her secret hopes. She met his gaze and tried to reassure him. "I'm okay. I'm not jumping out of airplanes or anything. I'm painting. Dr. Hill just said to make sure there was plenty of ventilation, which there is," she said, pointing to the open windows and the fan.

"I don't want you on the ladder."

She stifled a sigh. "Is this a testosterone thing?"

He looked at her for a long moment. "Yeah, it is." He pulled her toward him with a so-what-are-you-gonna-do-about-it expression on his face. "Stay off the ladder."

Overprotective. Stubborn. Hard man to love. Glory bit back a smile. "How was your day?"

As if he knew she was trying to divert him, his green eyes glinted with humor. "Better now that I know you're not getting back on that ladder."

Lord, he was persistent. She tried a different tack. "How's McAllister?" she asked, because she usually got an earful about Caleb's inept colleague.

"McAllister was put on earth to make me appreciate leaving work at the end of the day." He lifted his eyebrows. "Anything else you want to try before we settle the policy on the ladder?"

"Don't you think policy sounds a little retentive in this situation?"

"No."

He wasn't going to budge. "I want to finish the nursery this weekend," she said.

"I'll do the rest of it."

Sighing, she studied his taut face set in rigid lines and lifted her hand to his jaw. She was struck, as she often was, with the urge to soothe. "I wish you wouldn't worry. I promise to be careful."

She saw the struggle darken his eyes, and the depth of his emotion startled her. He pressed her hand to his lips. "You're important to me, Glory. You and the baby. If I could control the rotation of the planet, the weather, the intensity of heat from the sun, I'd do it. Keeping you safe is more essential to me than—" he shrugged "—than eating. I can't explain it. It feels primitive," he told her in a low, rough voice.

Swallowing hard over the knot in her throat, she shook her head. The ladder was just the tip of the iceberg, Glory realized. She'd watched that flash of fear come and go in his eyes and knew there was something deeper going on. She wished she could fix it, but she suspected that she wouldn't fully understand until Caleb did.

She cleared her throat. "Okay. No more ladder," she said, slipping her hands around to massage his tense neck muscles. "But I'm not budging on the ducks and bunnies."

Later that night she lay in his arms with his hands on her abdomen feeling the baby's kicks. It had become a nightly ritual. Glory had insisted it would help Caleb bond with the baby.

Although her theory was a little too touchy-feely for him, Caleb had never found it a hardship to hold Glory. Tonight the image of her falling from that ladder preyed on his mind. *What if she'd been hurt? What if the baby had been hurt?* Caleb had always been careful not to get close enough to another person to worry about them. Holding Glory tightly against him, he realized that was one more barrier she had blown to smithereens.

Every once in a while he took stock of the changes the marriage had made in him. Worrying, he decided with disgust, didn't go in the plus column.

"You're squishing me," she said in a muffled voice.

He took a deep breath and deliberately loosened his hold.

"Thanks. The ultrasound is scheduled for next week," she said, lifting her head to look at him. "Are you coming?"

"I wouldn't miss it."

She hesitated. "You want me to put a note on the refrigerator?"

He knew she was remembering the other doctor appointment when he hadn't shown up. "Yeah, but I won't forget this time."

"Good," she murmured, but the hint of uncertainty in her voice irritated him. She settled back down and sighed. "What was your father like?"

Caleb's lips twitched. Before they went to sleep, she often asked him questions. Usually about stuff he hadn't thought about in years. "Unlike my mother, he had average intelligence and a lot of common sense. When it was obvious that Eli and I had inherited my mother's intelligence, he was horrified we would end up being what he called 'smart dummies.'"

"So, what did he do with you?"

Caleb chuckled in remembrance. "Tried to teach us how to fix cars. Every Saturday morning," he said, shaking his head. "I was sure I'd die of boredom. I threw a lot of temper tantrums."

"Did he let you get away with it?"

"Yes and no. He let me vent. I think he understood my frustration. But he always told me that I'd gotten more than my share of brains and temper. So when I got upset, I shouldn't count to ten like other people and expect it to work. I should count to one hundred, and if that didn't help, I should repeat it."

Glory was quiet for a long moment. "Have you *ever* counted to a hundred when you're upset?"

Caleb laughed and squeezed her. "Once or twice."

"If we have a boy and he messes up your computer, what will you do?"

Caleb paused. "I'll tell you to take him outside and I'll swear for a few minutes. Then I'll put a lock on the door to my computer room and buy the kid his own computer."

"Hmm," she said, sounding impressed. "You know, if we end up with a smarty-pants kid, I'm really gonna need you."

"I'm glad to know I'll be of some use," he said dryly.

She jabbed him with her elbow. "Okay, big daddy. Here's another one for you. If we have a girl and she comes home late from a date with a love bite on her neck, what will you do?"

The scenario was pure speculation and it should have amused him, but Caleb felt his temper flare at the very thought. "I think you're gonna have to remind me to count."

"To one hundred?"

"More like one thousand."

Glory laughed and shifted to look at him again. The moon shone in the window, making her face glow. Her smile was soft, her eyes warm. "Are you going to be one of those terribly overprotective fathers?"

For Caleb, there was no other choice. "Terribly," he answered, but her questions had stirred a few within him. "What about you? What was your father like when you were growing up?"

"He worked a lot. He wasn't the primary disciplinarian," she said, seeming to choose her words with care. "My mother had a lot of influence over him."

"Henpecked, huh?"

She shot him a chastising look. "I didn't say that."

"Yes, you did," he told her with a grin. "In PR language. Besides, I saw her in action when they visited last month."

Glory sighed. "Mother can be—"

"Pushy as hell," he supplied.

"Extra assertive," she corrected. Her eyes rounded at the baby's firm kick. "Did you feel that?" she whispered.

"Yeah," he said, filled with the same sense of awe he saw on her face.

Another swift kick. She smiled. "I wonder whose temperament this child will end up with." She looked at Caleb and blinked. "What a terrifying thought."

He couldn't help laughing at her unedited remark and genuine dismay. She tried to backpedal, but he wouldn't let her, teasing her about bearing the *bad seed*.

After she went to sleep, however, his amusement waned and he lay wide awake, his hand folded around hers. Staring at her, he felt himself pulled in two different directions.

A secret voice inside him, quiet and deep, whispered, "Hold me closer. As close as you can get, sweetheart." But an older, stronger instinct urged him, "Back away, don't get too close. Don't care too much."

Chapter Thirteen

"Showtime," the ultrasound technician said with a smile, and motioned Glory into the examination room.

Glory mustered a halfhearted lifting of her lips in return. Caleb was late. He was going to miss it, and she was either going to cry or fantasize killing him in his sleep tonight with a broken laboratory beaker. Choosing the latter, she walked into the dimly lit room and got up on the table.

The technician glanced at her chart. "Your bladder nice and full?"

"Full," Glory said, uncomfortably aware of the water she'd just drunk.

The technician adjusted her robe, squirted a substance resembling gel on the scanner and looked at

Glory with sympathy. "It's cold," she warned, then put the scanner on Glory's abdomen.

Glory flinched, but one look at the screen and she was totally absorbed. The image wasn't crystal clear, but it was obviously a baby. Her baby. Her heart squeezed tight. "Oh, my goodness."

The door whipped open and Caleb burst into the room. "What did I miss?" Breathless and damp with perspiration, he looked like a wild man.

The technician frowned and straightened. "Excuse me, sir, but are you—"

"Husband. Father. Traffic was backed up, so I left my car on the street and ran the last—" He stared at the screen. "Oh, my God."

The technician chuckled. "Have a seat, and I'll tell you what you're seeing."

But Caleb was completely transfixed. Moving closer to the ultrasound monitor, he reminded Glory of a kid pressing his nose against the window of a candy store. She felt the baby move inside her, and watched a corresponding kick on the screen.

He turned to Glory and gave her a private killer smile. "Look what we did."

Her heart swelled in her chest at the expression on his face and, stretching her hand toward his, she decided to let him live.

"There's your bladder," the technician began. "If it's nice and full, we have an easier time identifying everything." She moved the slippery scanner over Glory's abdomen. "Your baby's head." She chuckled. "Looks like you've got a thumb-sucker on your hands."

Staring at the screen, Glory laughed. Sure enough, the baby's thumb was in its mouth. "And look," she said, "there's a foot."

"Yes, and there's the baby's spine. And that flicker is the heartbeat. Everything looks good so far." She moved the scanner. "Your placenta's a little low in the uterus," she murmured.

"Is that a problem?" Caleb asked, wanting everything to be perfect. If not perfect, normal. Completely and totally normal.

"Not really. It's not a placenta previa. Just something we like to keep track of," she said, making a note. "Let's take a measurement." She clicked a button and locked the frame, a metric ruler appearing on the screen. "Looks like you're right on schedule. Now," she said with a broad smile, "do you want to know the sex?"

Caleb and Glory answered at once.

"No," she said.

"Yes," he said.

"Yes," he repeated, certain he hadn't heard correctly.

"No," Glory insisted.

Completely confounded, he shook his head. "Of course we want to know," he said to the technician, then turned to Glory and tried to appeal to her feminine logic, *if such a thing existed*. "This way, you can tell everyone what you're having when they ask what you want for a gift.

"We can go ahead and pick out a name," he added, feeling a tinge of unease when her facial expression didn't change. "If we can know, then we want to know. When science offers an opportunity to eliminate the unknown, you always take it," he said firmly. "You never turn down information."

Glory sighed and patted his hand. "You're never going to understand this, darling, but I want it to be a surprise."

Thirty minutes later they left the doctor's office with two blurry photos. Glory had to give Caleb a ride back to work because his car had been towed. He nagged the living daylights out of her the entire drive.

"I can't believe you didn't want to know. The technician *knows,* for God's sake."

"And we will, too, in just a few months," she told him, determined to remain calm despite her antsy husband.

"I bet it's in your records," he went on.

"Maybe." She pulled to a stop in front of the lab.

"If I called your doctor this afternoon and agreed not to tell you—"

She met his gaze. "I would not be pleased."

He sighed, long and hard. Glory witnessed his unwilling surrender and almost changed her mind. But she couldn't. She tugged him closer and kissed him just like that sigh, long and hard. "We've made a miracle. This baby is like magic to me. He or she brought us together when I would have sworn we didn't have a chance."

She swallowed, hoping she was getting through, searching his face for a sign. "I know medical science can tell us all kinds of things, and I'm grateful for most of them." She lowered her voice to a whisper. "I just want to hang on to the magic and make it last a little longer. Can you try to understand?"

Seconds ticked past while he stared at her.

Glory felt the hum between them, the invisible connection that held her more tightly than words ever could.

"You drive me crazy," he told her in a rough voice, and kissed her with passion and gentleness. "Don't stop," he muttered, then got out of the car.

Caleb was later than usual the following night when he came home, but Glory didn't hold it against him. She was too delighted with the gifts from the surprise baby shower a co-worker had thrown for her.

When he came through the door, she gave him a quick hug and tugged him upstairs to the nursery as she often did these days. "You'll never believe all the gifts. Nighties and crib sheets and a cute little mobile with teddy bears. One of the women had a quilt made."

They walked into the room and Glory picked up the handmade gift with baby chicks and flowers and a big yellow sun. "Isn't it gorgeous? And Pat made an afghan. Feel it," she said, lifting it toward him. "It's so soft."

But Caleb just stood there in silence, wearing a slightly glazed expression.

In too good a mood to be frustrated, she kissed him on the cheek and smiled. "You have that here-but-not-here expression on your face. Have you heard anything I've said?"

Caleb blinked and backed away. "I heard everything. Nighties, crib sheets, mobile, quilt and afghan."

Feeling a tinge of uneasiness, Glory studied him. His hair was tied back with a leather cord today. His black shirt and pants seemed to reflect his mood. She looked at his eyes and saw frustration bordering on anger. His frustration she could handle, even his anger, but his remoteness unnerved her. Dropping the afghan into the crib, she asked, "Did something happen at the lab today?"

"Nothing unusual, but I have some work I need to do tonight. I'll probably be up late," he said, then turned and walked away.

Glory stared after him, an odd sense of dread crowding her chest. He'd come home a little glazed before, but she'd always been able to tease him out of it. And he'd never backed away when she kissed him. Something was wrong, but she wasn't sure if it was work related or if he was still upset over the ultrasound.

Folding the quilt and afghan, she tried to decide what to do. At a loss, she went downstairs and fixed him a sandwich.

"You're sure you're okay?" she asked, watching him as he stared at his computer screen. Fancy lay curled at his feet.

He nodded vaguely in response.

"Is there anything else I can get you?"

Focused on his task, he shook his head.

Troubled, Glory sighed and went to bed. Surprisingly, it didn't take her long to fall asleep, but around three in the morning she woke and Caleb still wasn't in bed. Pulling a robe around her now ample form, she crept downstairs to check on him. She found him staring out the picture window in the den, his shirt unbuttoned and his hands jammed in his pockets. He looked like a man fighting his demons. Glory wondered what was preying on him tonight.

She took a careful breath and walked closer to him. "Lots of stars out there tonight," she murmured.

He jerked his head toward her, then turned back to the window. "Yeah."

"Taking a break?" She touched his arm. His face was all set planes and angles unsoftened by the moonlight.

"I got sleepy, but I'm okay now."

"It's okay if you get a few hours of sleep tonight, isn't it?"

"Not tonight," he muttered, and turned away.

At a loss, Glory tightened her grasp. "Are you angry with me about something?"

He looked back at her for a long, heart-pounding moment. "No."

"Then what's going on?"

He shrugged. "Nothing. The research isn't moving as quickly as I'd like, so I'm putting in some more time."

"And nothing happened today?"

He sighed. "Not really. I just saw one of the letters today." He squinted at the clock on the mantel and made a wry face. "Yesterday," he corrected.

Glory shook her head. "One of the letters?"

"Yeah, from the speeches I gave. The lab's been getting letters since I came back, and I read one of them." His arm flexed beneath her touch, belying his casual tone. "Listen, I don't really have time to go into it right now—"

"It disturbed you," she concluded, wondering if someone had criticized him. "Were they nasty?"

He shook his head impatiently. "No, it was an Alzheimer's victim."

Glory needed a moment to digest that. "Oh."

He narrowed his eyes. "I need to get back to work. You go back to bed."

He moved away from her, and Glory felt her chest tighten painfully. "No."

He paused, his back still toward her. "No?"

She knitted her fingers together, not totally sure what to do, yet totally certain she couldn't just leave him to his own struggle. "I haven't seen you this upset in a long time, and I can't leave you this way."

He turned back to her, stiff and impatient. "You can't help."

Glory suffered from that hit, but did her best to hide it. "Maybe not, but this is what married people do for each other. If you're upset about something at work, it affects me. I need to be there for you when things aren't going well. I need you to be there for me, too."

"This isn't your concern," he told her firmly.

It was a little tougher not to flinch that time. "Yes, it is." She couldn't keep the emotion out of her voice. "It's about you, and I care about you, Caleb. I love you."

The room may have been dark, but her declaration was as blunt as bright sunlight. Looking as if she'd struck him, he dipped his head. "I don't want to care," he finally muttered. "I don't want to get letters from fifty-eight-year-old women who can't remember their children's names. I don't want to hear about how much they hope I find something. Fast," he said viciously. "Immediately. Before everything for them is gone."

Her heart splintered. Glory reached for him, but he shook his head and swore. "I don't want to care. It just gets in the way."

Glory shook her head slowly. "Oh, Caleb, you were born to care."

"No, I wasn't. I was born to use my mind to make life better for someone else. Caring isn't part of the equation," he told her. "Caring—" He broke off and swore again.

"Caring hurts," she whispered, and his head whipped up, his gaze latching on to hers. She lifted her hand to touch him again, then dropped it when she remembered he didn't want her that close. God, that hurt.

She blinked back tears. "You're the most intelligent man I know," she told him. "You *are* going to find this treatment, and then after that you will find another treatment that will fix another problem. And then you'll do it again," she told him, fighting the quiver in her voice. "You're the best kind of problem solver. But it's not just because you're so incredibly brilliant. It's because you care. More than your mind is involved."

Caleb shook his head. "Why are you saying this? Why—"

"Because it's true. More than your mind is involved. Your heart is. That's why I fell in love with you."

"You fell in love with a dream," he said, his anger spilling over. "I can't even tell you that I love you."

Glory's breath stopped. She felt as if he'd dealt her a mortal blow, and she had to fight to keep from doubling over. He was talking out of his own pain, she told herself. Caleb didn't deliberately hurt. It wasn't his nature. She made herself push past her own hurt, and for a sliver of a moment wondered where her new strength had come from. Just months before she would have been devastated. Somehow, some way, she had healed, and Caleb was partly responsible.

She took a step closer to him, seeing his wary gaze. "I know who I fell in love with, and it was you, Caleb Masters. You," she repeated, raising her voice. "You want to know why? Because you're more than a research machine. You care. And that's what makes you so special."

He pulled her into his arms, his green eyes glinting with passion as his gaze swept her face. "I don't know why you stick with me," he told her in a harsh whisper. "I don't want to care. Sometimes I don't want to care about you."

But he did. She could hear it in his voice, see it on his face, feel it in his body. Glory was so relieved he was holding her that tears rolled heedlessly down her face. "I keep hoping," she said in a broken voice, "I can love you well enough on the outside that you'll feel it on the inside." She squeezed him hard. "Caring hurts, Caleb. But caring makes you real."

Christmas came and went with Caleb fussing over Glory as she decorated the tree. Drawn into the activity in order to prevent her from using the ladder, he began to examine the ornaments and gradually seemed to enjoy himself. His remark that he couldn't recall when he'd last had a Christmas tree in his home twisted Glory's heart. On Christmas morning, though, he might as well have been twenty years younger when he opened the stocking Glory had stuffed for him.

His gift for her was an obscenely large diamond ring.

On New Year's Eve Glory stood alone in the bedroom. As she had for the past several days, she looked at the ring and just shook her head. For a man who was supposed to be practical and logical, this didn't fit.

The sound of Caleb's laughter rose from downstairs where he talked on the phone with his brothers. She glanced up and caught her reflection in the full-length mirror.

That person resembling the big red ball in Times Square simply could not be her.

Her first instinct was to glance away, but she made herself look. Fresh from the shower, she wore her robe. Her brown hair hung in damp waves to her shoulders. Her pregnancy had affected everything, even her face. Her fair complexion was tinted a dusky color from something her doctor called a pregnancy mask.

She tentatively lowered her gaze to her body. She would have killed for this bust line in high school, she thought with a wry smile, and lifted her hands to her full breasts. Skimming her hands over her considerable abdomen, she wondered if she would get her waist back. Thinking of the baby, she wondered if she would care.

In the past few weeks, when she looked in the mirror, Glory often felt as if she were looking at a stranger. She wondered what Caleb thought when he looked at her. Lately, they always made love in the dark.

She pushed open the robe.

"Andie said for us to make definite plans to bring that baby to their house next Christmas or she's going to—" Caleb broke off as he rounded the corner. Curious, he gave a half smile. "What are you doing?"

Feeling her cheeks heat, Glory pulled the robe closed and turned away from the mirror. "Nothing, really. I was just looking at how much I've grown," she said. "What else did Andie say?"

"Do you mind it?" he asked, coming closer to her.

"Mind what?"

"The changes. Getting bigger."

"I'm really excited about having the baby. I don't regret it one bit, but sometimes I feel a little..." She paused, trying to find the right word, and gave up. "Fat."

Caleb looked shocked. "You're joking."

"Well, I do weigh twenty pounds more,"she said, walking to the dresser to pull out some clothes. "And I look like I swallowed a watermelon."

Caleb came up behind her and wrapped his arms around her. "I like your body."

"You'll understand if I find that a little difficult to believe."

"No, I don't understand," he said, as if he was being logical and she wasn't. "This must be another woman thing. Come here." He led her back to the mirror and stood behind her. "Your face looks like it's glowing."

Self-conscious, Glory shook her head. "It's not really a glow. It's a ma—"

He cupped her cheek, breaking off her words with his touch. In the soft light of the bedside lamp, his gaze was dark and focused completely on her reflection. He slowly slid his palm from her cheek to her throat where her pulse tripped.

His gaze, possessive and masculine, met hers, and in that split second the atmosphere in the room changed. The air was charged with his need. Sensual awareness shimmered through her, and her embarrassment burned to ashes.

Her skin was acutely sensitive to his touch. Hot and tender like a sunburn. His chest provided a hard, warm brace against her back. Safe, yet his expression was dangerously male, sexually intent.

He trailed his hand down her chest inside the robe to her beaded nipples. Feeling his stroke all the way to her nether regions, she closed her eyes and bit her lip.

"I want you to watch," he murmured, nuzzling just behind her ear. "Open your eyes."

It was easier just to feel. It gave her a modicum of control. Looking was almost too much. Watching him watch her in the mirror, she felt wanted and wanton. Holding her breath, she forced her eyes open.

Caleb pushed her robe down. "Look at your breasts." As if he couldn't bear not to touch, he skimmed his hands over them, cupping them, gently squeezing and flicking his thumbs over her nipples.

His fondling gave her a buzz; she felt a tightening between her thighs. Suddenly it wasn't enough that he was touching her. She wanted to touch him. Arching her back, she slid her hand upward and threaded her fingers through his hair.

She heard him suck in a short breath. "Look," he urged, and pushed the robe from her completely. "Look at yourself in the mirror."

.Glory blinked at her reflection. Who was that woman? With her hand lifted to Caleb's cheek, her breasts jutted out proudly. Her belly was bare and rounded, her thighs slim in comparison. She looked ripe and provocative, voluptuous.

He slid his hand over her abdomen. "That's part of me inside of you," he said in a low, rough voice. "Do you know what that does to me?"

"What?" she whispered, not wanting to break the spell.

"It makes me want to get as close to you as I can." He dipped his lips to her throat and gently sucked her skin. He shifted his pelvis against her bare bottom and groaned. "It makes me want inside."

He plucked at one of her nipples again, and she undulated against him, instinctively seeking his hardness. "Why are you dressed?"

Caleb held her hips still and swore. "Give me a minute," he said, and tore at his buttons. One flew to the carpet, then he wrestled out of his shirt.

She circled around to kiss him and skimmed her hands over his chest. Her tongue teased and taunted until he was sweating. Fumbling with his belt, he unfastened his jeans and shoved them down with his briefs.

He had never witnessed a more arousing, erotic sight in his life than Glory naked and swollen with his baby. She was lush and everything beautiful that a woman could be, and she was his. He looked into her blue eyes, heavy with desire, and tried to get a grip on his overwhelming need at the same time that her full breasts glanced across his chest.

He shot out his hands to hold her still. "Just a minute," he said, kicking his jeans the rest of the way off.

But Glory was clearly in no mood to wait. Her wrists enclosed in his, she leaned forward and pressed an openmouthed kiss on his chest. His heart ricocheted against his rib cage.

She slid her tongue over his nipple. Her belly bounced against his.

His gut twisted at the dual sensation. "You gotta wait a—"

She met his gaze and his throat closed up. She looked hot and hungry, a little wild. For him. He'd seen her aroused before, but never with such uninhibited, shameless desire. It knocked him sideways. He loosened his grip on her wrists and she immediately flowed against him, all hot, womanly silk.

His skin rippled when her fingers cruised down his rib cage to his abdomen. Her avid mouth was everywhere—his lips, his throat, his shoulder.

Dizzy from the bombardment on his senses, he swore. A second passed and her hand wrapped around his hardness, immediately sending his pleasurable arousal into something far more urgent.

Stretching up on her toes, she curled against him, opening her thighs. Caleb pivoted his hips toward her, brushing her moistened femininity with his erection, but her belly kept him away. It wasn't close enough for either of them.

Glory made a little sound of frustration that undid him. Caleb bent to kiss her precious full abdomen. His heart clenched at the odd assortment of emotions clutching at him. "Turn around," he told her.

"But then I can't touch—"

"Just try it," he said and as soon as she turned, he bent his knees and slid against but not inside her. "Hot, wet, sweet," he muttered, and swept his hand around her thigh. He searched her giving folds and found her tiny nub of pleasure.

She moaned. "Oh, my," she murmured breathlessly, gliding against his throbbing hardness.

The movement of her bottom against his crotch was an irresistible invitation. Perspiration beaded his forehead. He curled a palm over one of her breasts and looked in the mirror. He swore again. Too much and not enough.

He muttered, "Hold on." Then he slid inside her, stroking her with his hand and erection, driving himself crazy with the sensation of her slick femininity.

Her gaze met his in the reflection of the mirror and he knew she was just as excited by the titillating sight of their lovemaking. She was nearly whimpering with pleasure. Her breath stopped. She stiffened and climaxed, crying out his name. Her knees buckled and her glazed eyes met his. "I'm sorry," she said in a thin voice as he caught her. "My legs—" She swallowed a sob. "I can't..."

His heart jerked at her distress. "It's okay," he murmured, holding her against him for a long moment while he throbbed with unspent passion. "It's okay," he said, as much to himself as her. He pulled her back toward the bed and tumbled her down on top of him.

She shifted and her breasts swayed in front of his face. Caleb's mouth went dry. "Show a little pity, Glory."

Before he'd finished her name, she sank onto him, enclosing him like a tight velvet fist. She met his gaze, and her siren smile wrapped around his heart and squeezed. Lowering her mouth to his, she contracted her inner muscles around him in an intimate hug and Caleb reached for the ceiling.

When he could see straight, he swore. "What was that?"

"Just one of those pregnancy things," she said, and kissed him.

"Pregnancy th—" She did it again and he bucked.

Glory laughed. The sound was deliciously wicked. "Kegel exercises. My doctor says I should do a hundred a day." She smiled. "Ready for number three?"

"A hundred! Damn, I don't—"

She did it again and Caleb threw in the towel. He thrust inside her as deep as he could go. She gave him a French kiss that made steam come out of his ears, all the while clenching his aching masculinity. Around number ten he lost it, mind, body and soul. And losing had never felt so good.

Six weeks later Caleb rushed down the hall to the hospital auditorium. *The movie.* Glory had been talking about this for weeks. They'd finished the prepared childbirth classes, and Caleb could explain and demonstrate all the different breathing techniques used during moderate labor, transition and resisting the urge to push.

Ash had laughed his butt off when Caleb had tried to tell him there actually was a difference between panting and focused breathing. His younger brother was enjoying Caleb's current state of upheaval. Every time he called, he mentioned the "three little words" Caleb ought to be saying to Glory. Caleb usually terminated the discussion by passing the phone to Glory.

He wondered if his reluctance to declare his love had something to do with giving up control or surrendering his autonomy. Frowning, he shook his head as he rounded a corner. He didn't know the answer, and he sure as hell didn't have time to wallow in his uncertainty.

He pushed open the door and entered the class. The instructor greeted him in a long-suffering tone. He supposed he'd earned that. He'd been late to every class.

"Hello, Dr. Masters. We've just finished our review of breathing techniques and early signs of labor. We'll begin the film now." She gestured toward Glory. "Your wife's here on the front row if you'd like to join her."

He nodded and sat beside her.

Glory took his hand. "I think you're her favorite," she whispered.

"What's not to love," Caleb said dryly. "How long is the movie?"

She shot him a quelling look. "You just got here."

"It was just a question."

"Probably at least an hour. It's supposed to show *everything*," his sweet, adorable wife said with uncharacteristic relish.

The room darkened. Caleb stifled a sigh and shifted to find a comfortable position. He would just switch into scientist mode while he watched this, he told himself. He hadn't been nearly as excited at the prospect of seeing this movie as Glory had, although, for the life of him, he couldn't say why.

He knew giving birth was a natural event in most women's lives. Although it was extremely taxing on a woman's body, most seemed to come through it just fine. He was certain Glory would, too.

The film opened with a woman in the early stages of labor. With her husband beside her, she walked the hospital corridor outside her birthing room. As the instructor had told the class, her discomfort didn't appear to require anesthetic or the use of breathing techniques.

Using a time-lapse approach, labor progressed with increasing discomfort. Caleb grew suspicious of the term *discomfort* when the woman in the movie started screaming.

Reality hit him hard. He tightened his hand around Glory's. This was going to happen to her. She was going to go through labor. She was going to suffer incredible pain.

He found himself breathing with the couple in the movie. He pictured Glory in the hospital gown, screaming in pain, and felt himself go light-headed.

He watched in horror as the doctor made the woman put her feet in some sort of stirrup contraptions that looked like something out of the Dark Ages.

The baby's head crowned, and Caleb distantly heard the excitement of his fellow classmates. His own excitement was diminished, however, with the close-up of the doctor cutting the episiotomy.

The doctor was going to cut Glory.

He saw the blood, and his stomach rolled. From his reading, he knew a woman usually lost only one unit of blood during a normal delivery, but it sure as hell looked like a lot more. Caleb looked at the blood-stained cloths and bloodstained plastic gloves. He closed his eyes.

Glory nudged him with her elbow. "Look, you're gonna miss it."

Bracing himself, he watched in appalled fascination as the bloodstained baby pushed through the woman's opening and was delivered. The camera zoomed in on the delivery of the placenta and the doctor stitching up the episiotomy.

By that time the room was swimming in front of his eyes. He pulled his trembling hand from Glory's and wiped his clammy forehead. For a terrible moment he wondered if he was going to faint or puke.

Desperation sent him to his feet.

Glory stared up at him. "What are you doing?"

Caleb locked his knees to keep from pitching forward. "I'll be back in a couple of minutes," was all he could manage before he raced from the room, down the corridor and out the exit.

Cold air hit his face with the same effect as smelling salts. He drank in long, deep breaths and leaned weakly against the concrete wall.

When his rational mind regained control again, he shook his head. Ash would be howling with laughter if he could see him now. God, he felt like an idiot. For Pete's sake, he'd cut open a pig in anatomy class in college, and now he couldn't watch a labor-and-delivery movie.

He thought of Glory and his heart wrenched.

Sweet, adorable, very pregnant Glory.

The woman had wrecked him.

Chapter Fourteen

It was two days after her due date, and Glory was cranky. Unaccustomed to her size, she'd developed an embarrassing tendency to bump into people. She said "excuse me" so frequently she'd begun to say it to the furniture when she bounced into it. A full night's sleep was a mere memory. Her darling baby seemed to have found a permanent resting place on her bladder.

Sighing, she prepared for bed and reassured herself that it would be over soon. She felt the baby kick, and smiled, putting her hand on her abdomen. Despite her discomforts, the thought of holding her baby still caused a stir of excitement inside her.

"Ready for bed?" Caleb asked, coming into their bedroom.

"Guess so," she murmured, putting down her

hairbrush. "It's still pretty early. If you've got work to do, you don't have to come to bed now."

Caleb shook his head. "Oh, no. If I don't get sleepy, I can just make a few notes in bed."

Glory smiled. He'd begun to hover, making sure she got as much sleep as she could, making sure she felt safe. He'd even started calling her a couple of times each day from the lab. The conversations weren't always coherent, but she adored him for making the effort. "How was your day?" she asked, and walked over to unbutton his shirt. Sex was nearly out of the question, but she still liked touching him.

Caleb twisted his mouth in a half smile. "Good. McAllister's on vacation. How about you?"

"Good," she said. "I'm taking your advice and cutting back on my schedule a little. I'm not going in tomorrow."

Caleb gave her a quick kiss in approval and ditched the rest of his clothes.

"I bought a book for the baby today."

"I thought you already had one on infant care."

She picked up the illustrated children's book from her nightstand. "I do. This is for us to read to the baby. I can't remember a time when I didn't love having my parents read to me."

Caleb gave her a blank look.

Glory felt a dart of surprise. "Your parents *did* read to you, didn't they?"

He shrugged. "Yeah. My mother read *War and Peace* and Homer's *Odyssey.*"

"When you were a teenager?"

Caleb shook his head. "No, I think I was about five."

She didn't know whether to laugh or weep. "Tell me you didn't miss *The Little Engine That Could* and *The Poky Little Puppy*."

He shot her a wary look. "You're not going to cry if I tell you I did, are you?"

"No," she said, disconcerted that he could read her so well.

"Good. I can honestly say I don't recall either of those titles. Have I been deprived?" he asked dryly.

"Yes, you have, and I think we should start correcting this problem right away. Your bedtime story tonight is my all-time favorite *The Velveteen Rabbit*, by Margery Williams."

Wearing nothing but white briefs and a sexy smile, he strolled toward her and kissed her long and hard. "I like grown-up bedtime stories better."

"I know you do. That's why I have a future gymnastics champion inside me jumping up and down on my bladder."

"It's not a gymnastics star," he told her seriously. "It's a trapeze artist. Our child will grow up and join the circus."

Glory shuddered and held up a hand. "Stop. You'll give me nightmares."

Caleb chuckled and sank onto the bed. "Okay. Go ahead and read. Is this a sissy book?"

She shot him a dark look. "This is my favorite book in the world," she told him in a reverent voice, "and I know you'll love it."

"PR talk for shut up and listen," Caleb quipped, and Glory punched him.

In the soft lamplight Glory leaned back against her pillow and began to read the story of the toy rabbit stuffed full of sawdust. Caleb listened to her voice and thought about how lucky their child would be to have Glory as a mother, to hear her read and murmur good-night every night.

Surprisingly engaged by the toy rabbit's quest to become *real,* Caleb listened intently. In the toy hierarchy, it appeared that the rabbit was on the bottom rung. There was always the hope, however, that he could become real, but the rabbit feared losing his fur and eyes in order to become real, and initially found sleeping in the boy's bed very uncomfortable.

Glory paused as she eased farther down in the bed.

After a while she yawned and read about how the rabbit was so happy with the little boy that he didn't notice he was losing his fur.

She read a couple more pages and yawned again. Then her voice faded and dropped off halfway through the book.

Caleb muffled his chuckle when he saw that she'd fallen asleep. As she'd often told him lately, she was "sleeping for two." Not wanting to wake her, he arranged the covers and carefully pulled the book from her lap. Sighing in her sleep, she rolled on her side.

He almost put the book aside on the nightstand, but curiosity about how the story ended made him read farther. The point of the story was both simple and complex. The little boy's love had made the rabbit real, and becoming real was a painful but rewarding process. Logically Caleb knew a sawdust rabbit could never become real because a little boy loved him and a fairy kissed him. It was scientifically impossible. It must have been the late hour, but the message struck a chord in him.

Before Glory, Caleb's life had been intense, but simple and focused. For all intents and purposes, he'd functioned as a research machine. With the exception of his immediate supervisor, most people he saw on a daily basis had come to expect that of him.

Now he was human.

He glanced at Glory and frowned. When had it happened? She'd rubbed away his defenses by loving him, and she'd made him care even when it hurt.

Caleb flipped back to an earlier passage in the book and read it again.

"Does it hurt?" asked the Rabbit.

"Sometimes," said the Skin Horse, for he was always truthful. "When you are Real you don't mind being hurt."

"Does it happen all at once, like being wound up," he asked, "or bit by bit?"

"It doesn't happen all at once," said the Skin Horse. "You become. It takes a long time. That's why it doesn't often happen to people who break easily, or have sharp edges or who have to be carefully kept. Generally, by the time you are Real, most of your hair has been loved off, and your eyes drop out and you get loose in the joints and very shabby. But these things don't matter at all, because once you are Real you can't be ugly, except to people who don't understand."

Caleb pondered the message for a long moment. Glory had always understood that he was more than his research.

He shook his head and closed the book. If he told anyone in the lab he shared some similarities with *The Velveteen Rabbit,* they'd have him committed, but Caleb knew it had happened. Glory was making him real.

And what he felt for her was more than care and more than need.

It was love.

His heart swelled with the realization. Both freeing and alarming, the knowledge burst through his veins and spread through his entire body.

He stared at Glory. Who would have thought she could have done that to him? He wanted to tell her right that moment, to wake her up and tell her over and over, to see her smile.

He opened his mouth and hesitated, seeing the blue circles of fatigue under her eyes. She was exhausted. For once in his life he decided to show a little restraint and tell her tomorrow when he came home from work. "I love you," he whispered, the words feeling awkward and new. He wondered if he would ever get used to saying them.

In the semisleep of morning Glory rolled over and heard a crunching sound. She frowned, and searched beneath the covers. Her fingers encountered a crumpled little piece of paper. She gave a rusty laugh, knowing full well what it was.

Lifting the paper above the bedspread, she squinted at the chemical equation scratched on it. Caleb must have had a tough time going to sleep, she mused. She hoped he wasn't worried about anything. Sighing, she lay still for a moment, feeling the baby wiggle a little.

Her abdomen tightened in one of the Braxton-Hicks—false labor—contractions she'd had throughout the pregnancy. She waited for it to pass, then scooted out of bed.

In a burst of energy, she spent the morning cleaning out a closet. By lunchtime she was rubbing the dull ache in her back. The sunny day lured her outside and she took a long walk and chatted with Timmy for a few minutes. He was excited because his mother had *finally* decided he was old enough for his own cat. So he wouldn't have to share Fancy with Caleb anymore, although he assured Glory he would continue to give Fancy treats and pet her.

Glory figured Fancy would be pleased with that news. In PR terms, the cat was weight enhanced. As Glory returned to the house, she noticed her backache hadn't gone away. It had intensified into a rhythmic tightening. After timing the cramps for an hour, she let out a scream of happiness that sent Fancy scrambling under the bed.

Glory was finally in labor.

Since she was concerned about rush hour traffic, Glory insisted on driving herself to the hospital. Caleb argued with her in increasing volume, until she politely said she really had to go and *hung up on him.*

In a full sweat, Caleb entered the hospital swearing without ceasing. He tugged at his collar and went after the admitting clerk. "I'm looking for my wife. She's in labor. Her name is Glory Masters," he added when the clerk looked at him blankly. "Where is she?"

The clerk lifted his hand. "Just a moment, sir." He punched some buttons on the computer. "She hasn't been ad—"

Caleb swore. "I knew I shouldn't have let her drive. I tried to reason with her. Have you ever tried to reason with a pregnant woman? It's futile. Totally fu—"

"Hi, honey," Glory said breathlessly with an excited smile. "Ready to have a baby?"

Caleb's chest tightened at the sight of her. She looked so damn pleased with herself. "You okay? Let me take the suitcase."

He reached for it, but she shook her head. "What I'd really like you to do is park my car. I left it in a no-parking zone, and then I guess we need to go through admission and—"

"I'll take care of that," Caleb told her, and within a minute he commandeered an aide with a wheelchair to take her upstairs.

His adrenaline was pumping by the time he met her in the Labor and Delivery area. Dressed in a hospital gown, she was walking in the hallway. As he approached, he watched her stop and take deep breaths. "Are you sure you don't want to stick closer to the bed?" he asked.

"And lie there like a beached whale?" She shook her head. "I want to walk as long as I can. That way, I'll at least have gravity on my side. And you remember what I said about painkillers," she told him with a serious expression. "I don't want to be out of it when the baby's born."

"Okay," he said reluctantly. He wasn't looking forward to seeing Glory in pain. "What'd the doctor say?"

"I'm four and a half centimeters dilated," she said, continuing to walk slowly. "The baby's heartbeat is fine. They took some of my blood and will hook me up to an IV in a while." She gave him a searching glance. "Are you okay?"

Taken aback that she would ask, he shrugged. "Of course." He shoved his hands into his pockets. "I'm not the one in labor."

Her mouth lifted in a secret smile, and she leaned closer to kiss him. "I'm so glad you're here. It makes me feel more secure. Do you mind walking with me?"

In the overall scheme of things it was an insignificant assignment, but Caleb was relieved to have something to do. Over the following hours his respect for Glory grew with each passing contraction. He didn't like to admit it, but if he'd been the one in labor, he would have been screaming at the nurse for an epidural hours ago. Glory, instead, used the breathing techniques and stayed on her feet until she just couldn't manage it anymore.

The birthing room was a strong contrast against the sterility of the rest of the hospital. He distantly noted the colorful curtains and television, but was more comforted by the sight of the fetal heart monitor and the fact that a fully equipped operating room was next door.

He never felt useless. He'd expected to, but when she asked him to hold her hand, she made it seem as if it were the most important gesture in the world.

Her water broke, and the nurse examined her and set up an IV drip. When she left, Glory looked at him. "It's going to get worse now. Did you bring some paper or something to write on?"

"Write what?" Caleb asked in confusion.

"Well, one of your chemistry equations or something."

He looked at her in disbelief. "Do you really think I could concentrate on that right now?"

"You're going to have to concentrate on something. It's going to get worse," she repeated. Another contraction hit, and she went into transition.

Caleb braced himself for the screaming, but she didn't yell or curse at him. He almost wished she would. She bit her lip so hard it bled, and occasionally gave little moans that broke his heart into tiny pieces. He was stunned by her stamina, but he grew concerned when she seemed to grow progressively weary in a short time, so he called the nurse.

She checked Glory's progress and the baby's heartbeat. This time, though, she frowned as she looked at the monitor.

Caleb felt a sliver of unease. "Something wrong?"

"The baby's heartbeat is a little low," she said. "I thought it might just be this machine, but we'd better bring Dr. Hill in." She turned to Glory. "How are you feeling, Mrs. Masters?"

Glory had lost her color. "I feel a little faint." Her face tightened in a grimace of pain. "I really want to be awake for the birth," she told her, her voice trembling. "What's wrong with the baby?"

The nurse patted her arm. "We don't know. That's why I'm getting the doctor. I'll be back in just a minute."

"Caleb." She squeezed his hand tightly, her wide, distressed eyes meeting his. "Something's wrong. I know it. Something terrible is going to happen."

"Nothing is going to happen. You're going to be fine," he insisted. At the same time, he was fighting his own rising alarm. *Why was she so pale?*

Tears welled in her eyes. "Please don't let anything happen to the baby. Please don't—"

"Her blood pressure," Dr. Hill told the nurse as she entered the room and put on gloves. She frowned at the heart rate registered on the monitor, then examined Glory. "You're almost fully dilated, but you're bleeding too much."

Caleb's gut clenched.

"Blood pressure's sixty over forty," the nurse said.

"She's going into shock," Dr. Hill said. "We're doing a section. Move her now." The doctor murmured a few words of encouragement to Glory he couldn't hear.

"You'll have to stand back," the nurse told him when he tried to keep holding Glory's hand.

The atmosphere in the birthing room shifted from peacefulness to urgency. In seconds the room was filled with people prepping Glory, then wheeling her to surgery. Before he could comfort her, they'd slipped an oxygen mask on her. Shoved aside, Caleb fought a cold knot of terror.

"Dammit, be careful!" he kept saying, but no one listened. He tried to get to Glory, but the aide rolling her bed into the hall shook his head.

"What's going on?" Caleb demanded, racing after the doctor.

"Your wife is hemorrhaging, and the baby's heart rate is dangerously low. We have to do an emergency cesarean." Sympathy shadowed her features as she stopped just outside the operating room. "I'm sorry, but you'll have to wait outside."

Outside! Away from Glory? Every fiber of his being protested. "No, I can't leave her. She—"

Dr. Hill shook her head. "We can't allow you in during emergency surgery. Hospital policy. I'll give you news as soon as I can." She pushed through the doors.

He started after her. "But—"

A nurse stopped him. "You *must* wait outside."

He overheard another nurse inside the operating room. "Mom's blood pressure's down to fifty over thirty. Baby's heart rate is under ninety."

The door slid closed in front of his face. It's not just a generic *mom,* he wanted to yell at the nurse. It's Glory. My Glory. Our baby.

He stood there, his body and soul straining to be with her while they operated. It was all he could do not to burst in there, but he didn't want to distract the doctor. "Excuse me," an aide gently asked, "is that your wife in surgery?"

Caleb nodded, dazed.

"Come with me. I know a place where you can wait."

He reluctantly followed. It wasn't logical, but he thought Glory would be okay if he stayed as close to her as possible. Caleb was beginning to think he'd never been completely logical about Glory because he'd been in love with her since he'd met her again. God knows, love didn't make a man logical.

What if he lost her? Pain wrenched at him and his heart nearly stopped. Sitting on the vinyl couch with a cup of vending-machine coffee in his hand, he began to shake. He set the untouched coffee on the table.

She couldn't die. His mind and heart denied the possibility. What would his life be like without her now? What would it be like to go through a day without her smile? Without being asked, "How was your day?" Without being *loved* the way she loved him.

She'd turned his life upside down, but Caleb had learned to like it that way. She wore him out enough that he didn't have as much trouble sleeping as he used to. She'd added color and texture and challenged him. She'd made him care again. She'd made him love.

And he'd never told her how much he loved her.

He closed his eyes at the sharp slice of truth. His throat closed up. His chest was a vise of pain. The possibility that she could die never knowing tore him up. *God, what can I do?* he prayed as he'd never prayed before, ready to bargain and beg. Whatever it took.

A litany of prayers racing through his mind, he lifted his hand and rubbed his face, feeling a disconcerting moisture on his cheeks. Astonished, Caleb couldn't remember the last time he'd cried. Unable to contain his desperation, he began to weep.

Pulling himself together, Caleb took a few deep breaths and shook his head. Becoming *real,* he decided, hurt like hell. He wiped his face, then squeezed his forehead. He stared down at the patch of floor in front of him, and a pair of rain-sodden boots stepped into view.

Caleb's gaze moved up drenched jeans, a wet leather jacket, a big hand clutching a teddy bear, the other holding a motorcycle helmet, to his brother Ash's familiar face. "It was raining just south of here," he said, explaining his wet appearance. "They said I'd find you here. How bad is it?" he asked, sitting next to Caleb. He set his helmet on the table.

"Bad. She's hemorrhaging. The baby's heart rate was low."

Ash grimaced. "Sorry, bro. Andie and Eli told me to tell you they'll be here this weekend. I came as soon as I got your message on the answering machine when Glory first went into labor this afternoon."

"You didn't have to," Caleb said, but his brother's presence comforted him.

"Yeah. I did."

"Thanks," Caleb said, and took a deep breath. "I don't know what I'll do if something happens to her."

"Maybe you won't have to know."

"I never told her I loved her."

Ash sighed. "Maybe you'll get another chance." His gaze met Caleb's. "I wouldn't waste any time telling her next time you see her."

He wouldn't, Caleb thought. If he got another chance.

A nurse pushed open the door with a bundle in her arms. "Mr. Masters?"

His heart in his throat, he stood immediately. "Here. Glory? How is Glory?"

Her face was filled with sympathy. "It was an abruption. Your wife had a very difficult time, and she lost a lot of blood."

He hung suspended in time. "But she's okay," he said in a gruff voice. *She had to be okay.* "She's going to be okay. Right?"

She nodded. "Yes. It was a good thing Dr. Hill acted so quickly. She's finishing up with Mrs. Masters right now." The nurse checked her watch. "Your wife should be in Recovery within a few minutes."

Relief made him light-headed. His heart was hammering a mile a minute. He would hold her again. He would tell her how much he loved her. "She's okay," he said, and Ash squeezed his shoulder.

The nurse smiled. "In the meantime, meet your daughter. Eight pounds and nine ounces. Her first Apgar score was only five, but she perked up with a little oxygen. Her second score was eight."

"Eight?" Ash echoed, leaning over Caleb's shoulder to take a peek. "She looks like a ten to me."

The Apgar score, Caleb recalled absently from his reading, was a system of evaluating infants in different areas such as heart rate and respiration. His mind was racing. Five was fair. Eight was good.

Glory was okay.

Caleb stared at his daughter's face, and everything inside him stopped. Her little mouth was pursed, and her tiny nose tilted up slightly just the way Glory's did. Her eyes were closed. Her forehead was crinkled in a frown. Her perfectly round head was perfectly bald. His heart gave a jerk. She was the most beautiful baby ever born.

"Would you like to hold her?"

"Yeah," he said, automatically extending his arms. The soft weight of his daughter was delivered to him. The impact of the moment was shocking, life-changing. How had Glory known? *This baby is like a miracle*. Glory's words played back to him. *She brought us together when I would have sworn we didn't stand a chance.*

Full of all the emotions he'd tried to deny, he stared, speechless, at their precious miracle. He felt a bittersweet ache that he couldn't share this slice of time with Glory. Snapping out of his daze, he looked up at the nurse.

"I need to see my wife."

She shook her head. "We don't usually allow anyone in—"

"Please."

She must have sensed his desperation. "She's going to be very groggy," she warned him, and hesitated. "Maybe we can make an exception this time. Come upstairs in thirty minutes, and I'll see what I can do."

Caleb looked at Ash, then back to his baby, and felt the sting of tears for the second time that day. He stared at his daughter in wonder for a few more minutes, then went upstairs to wait impatiently outside the recovery room.

Dr. Hill made a quick appearance and reassured him about Glory's prognosis, but he wanted to see for himself that she was alive, that she would be okay. Ash waited with him, and Caleb had never been more grateful for a brother's support. "Thanks for coming. It means a lot."

Ash shrugged. "Wouldn't miss it," he said, and they grinned at each other.

The nurse, however, wasn't grinning when she refused to allow Caleb to take the baby into Recovery with him.

"It's the least we can do since she was knocked out during the birth of her first child," Caleb argued.

"We don't allow babies in Recovery."

"Maybe you should," he told her. "Maybe your patients would *recover* more quickly."

"This is *extremely* unusual," she said, clearly regarding him as a pain.

"So is an abruption," he persisted, accustomed to being regarded as a pain.

She gave a long sigh and lifted her hands in surrender. "Okay. Five minutes."

Ash snickered. "You were always world-class at arguing."

Caleb followed the woman through the doors of the recovery room to Glory where she lay incredibly still, incredibly pale. His chest tightened in alarm. "You're sure she's—"

"She's going to be fine," the nurse assured him. "She's just had a rough time."

The nurse allowed him a few moments of privacy with her. "That's your mom," he told his daughter. "And let me tell you, you are one lucky kid."

Glory stirred. "Caleb," she whispered, working her eyelids, but not quite opening them.

Holding the baby in one arm, he enclosed Glory's hand in his. "It's me. I'm here. I—"

She opened her mouth to speak again and he bent closer. "How many..." She swallowed. "How many trucks ran over me?" she asked in a rusty voice.

Caleb chuckled, but his gut twisted. "Too many. I brought your baby girl to see you."

She smiled, her eyelids still heavy. "The baby? They told me she was okay." She blinked several times, then focused on the face of their sleeping daughter. "Oh,

Caleb, she's beautiful. Don't you think she's beautiful?"

"Yeah, she's beautiful," he said, his heart swelling so that he thought it would burst.

"I wish I could hold her."

Caleb looked at the assorted IV's and equipment surrounding Glory and shook his head. "In a little bit. I promise." He cleared his throat. "Glory, there's something I need to tell you. Something I should have told you a long time ago, but I didn't realize it until last night when you were sleeping."

Her eyes were growing heavy again. She wrinkled her eyebrows in a twinge of pain. "What is it?"

Caleb saw that she was fading fast, and was determined to tell her. "I love you. I really love you."

"Oh." Closing her eyes, Glory smiled and squeezed his hand. "I already knew that."

Epilogue

Caleb had given her roses once a week since the baby was born and told her he loved her several times a day. He kissed her tenderly, held her tight . . . and yelled at her when she did too much.

Glory rolled over in bed. It was early, early morning and Caleb was rocking Miss Melissa Masters back to sleep after Glory had nursed her. She wouldn't be surprised if he was reading *The Velveteen Rabbit* to Melissa. He read it so often the poor child would probably have the story memorized by the time she was six months old.

He must have coaxed her to sleep a little faster this time, she thought, hearing Caleb's footsteps just as he rounded the corner. She smiled up at him. "Good thing my parents and your brothers are gone," she said, referring to his nearly nude body.

He slid between the covers and pulled her against him. "Are you complaining?"

She kissed his neck and nuzzled against him. "Not me. Did the queen finally decide to go to sleep?"

"Yeah, she seemed a little..."

Glory bit her lip in amusement. When it came to his daughter's more challenging personality traits, Caleb was a master at understatement. "Fussy?" she prodded.

"Well..."

"I thought you were going to punch Ash when he called her a screaming meemie."

Caleb frowned. "She's verbally precocious."

Glory burst out in laughter. "She's got colic."

"Are you trying to tell me my daughter's not perfect?" he asked, pulling Glory on top of him.

"Not me."

His face turned serious. "I love you."

Her heart swelled. It always did when he said the words. She kissed his chin and clung to the hard strength of his shoulders. Sometimes the honesty of his commitment was so real and powerful it was hard for her to take it in.

"It occurs to me that it's been six weeks since I first told you I love you," he said, slipping his hands possessively down her body. "Six weeks where we've been inundated with visitors. Your doctor gave you the go-ahead for *everything* yesterday, didn't he?"

"Yes." Glory saw the raw glint of need in his green eyes and felt a sweet surge of affection and desire. He never let her doubt that she made him burn, that she was the one he would always want.

"I think it's past time for a physical demonstration." He rubbed his lips down her throat, sending her pulse skittering. "Her majesty is asleep." He rolled them gently to their sides. "And I've been—"

They both stopped at the crackling sound. Glory stared at Caleb for a breathless moment and groaned. "Please tell me that's not what I think it is."

She searched beneath the covers and pulled out the scrap piece of paper. She recognized Caleb's familiar scrawl, but she couldn't have explained the chemical equation if her life had depended on it.

"Before you get wound up, check the other side," he told her.

Glory turned the piece of paper over and smiled at the three words written on the back. She realized she could live with finding scrap papers in the bed for the rest of her life as long as they were Caleb's. She lifted her face to his and whispered his words right back to him. "I love you, too."

* * * * *